BLUE★STAR
RAPTURE

BLUE★STAR RAPTURE

JAMES W. BENNETT

ALADDIN PAPERBACKS

New York London Toronto Sydney Singapore

I wish to thank my editors at Simon & Schuster, David Gale and Michael Conathan, for their productive and prompt editorial suggestions, which helped make *Blue Star Rapture* a better book. I am also indebted to fellow author Nancy Brokaw, whose ongoing perceptions about this book and my other manuscripts are a consistent blessing.

First Aladdin Paperbacks edition March 2001
Text copyright © 1998 by James W. Bennett

Aladdin Paperbacks
An imprint of Simon & Schuster
Children's Publishing Division
1230 Avenue of the Americas
New York, NY 10020

Also available in a Simon & Schuster Books for Young Readers hardcover edition.
Designed by Paul Zakris.

The text of this book was set in 11-point Sabon.
Printed and bound in the United States of America
10 9 8 7 6 5 4 3 2 1

The Library of Congress has cataloged the hardcover edition as follows:
Bennett, James W.
Blue Star rapture / by James W. Bennett.
p. cm.
Summary: While attending a high-profile basketball camp, T.J. begins to re-think both his motivations and his actions in guiding his learning-disabled but athletically gifted friend through the college recruitment process.
ISBN: 0-689-81580-8 (hc.)
[1. Motivation (Psychology)—Fiction. 2. Honesty—Fiction.
3. Basketball—Fiction. 4. Camps—Fiction.] I. Title.
PZ7.B43989B1 1998
[Fic]—dc21
97-15549
ISBN: 0-689-84150-7 (Aladdin pbk.)

THIS BOOK IS DEDICATED TO THE MEMORY
OF MY MOTHER, MARGARET RUTH MORRIS,
THE BEST PARENT A BOY COULD EVER HAVE.

BLUE★STAR
RAPTURE

ONE

ON the day they left for the Full Court basketball camp, T.J. was flat on his back on the concrete, cramped beneath the deteriorating Toyota. While the grease streaked his chin and rust flakes stung his eyes, he struggled with the bolts on the starter bracket. Tyron, who was supposed to be helping him, was instead power slamming the basketball through the old rim on the older garage. "Hawkeyes!" he cried each time. "Ass-kickin' Hawkeyes!"

Every now and then, T.J. hollered at him to come and pass a wrench under, or a bolt, or a screwdriver. Each time, Tyron asked him, "Is it fixed yet?"

"No," said T.J. "It'll get fixed a lot faster if

you stay here to help me instead of playin' Hawkeye over there."

"Boring."

"Did you know that next to the battery the starter is the heaviest engine part there is?"

"No," Tyron answered. "Have you ever been to Carver-Hawkeye?"

"I've never been there. I've seen it on TV. It's a huge arena, but what else would you expect from a Big Ten university?"

"Sellouts, you mean. ESPN, huh?"

"I don't want to talk about it. They sent you a letter, that's all. Coaches send letters to lots of players, they work from a huge mailing list. Haven't you figured that out yet?"

"Maybe they'll offer me a scholarship, though."

"Maybe a lot of stuff. Let's just kiss off on this Hawkeye shit, okay? North State was in on you from the beginning; if there's going to be a chance, that's probably where it will be. Either that or junior college." T.J. tried to take a deep breath, but all he got for that was a mouth full of rusty granules. "This isn't the one," he said to Tyron. "I told you the *crescent* wrench."

"Slam-dunkin' Hawkeyes, man!"

Tyron jumped to his feet; after two or three of his giant strides, he was ready for another assault on the basket. The bolts were loose, so the rim wavered like a wire coat hanger. By turning his head to the side, T.J. was able to watch Tyron's drama. "You'll break the rim off if you don't watch it," he said.

"No hangin' and no jacknifin'," Tyron replied. "Only power dunks."

"Come get me that big screwdriver."

When he passed it under, he said, "Explain to me about Proposition Forty-eight."

"No. We've tried that before."

"Okay then, explain to me Prop forty-two."

T.J. had had it up to his eyeballs with all the talk he'd heard about Propositions 42 and 48 from Lindsey, the coach at North State, and others. The propositions were the combination of high school grades and standardized test scores you had to achieve to become eligible for a college basketball scholarship. At times, he himself was confused by it all, so how could he explain it to someone else? To *Tyron?* "The bottom line is, you've got to study hard and get good grades."

"Shit."

"You asked."

Tyron's response to this was another slam dunk and another cry of "Hawkeyes! In your face, motherfucker!"

As soon as the starter was bolted firmly in place, T.J. crawled out from under the car. He flexed his torso to work some of the stiffness from his back while wiping grease from his hands and face. With his toe he kicked the tools out from underfoot.

Gaines, the sportswriter from the *Ledger-Daily,* was sitting on his front porch. *How long has he been sitting there?* T.J. asked himself.

"Is it fixed yet?" Tyron asked T.J. while ignoring the sportswriter altogether.

"It's fixed. Go get your stuff."

The big guy didn't have to be told twice. He headed down the block in an up-tempo jog.

"Hey, Nucci." The sportswriter was calling him. T.J. wondered why Gaines's clothes never seemed to work. He was wearing a pair of royal blue walking shorts, but with black socks and white canvas deck shoes. He asked T.J., "How close does he live?"

"Less than a block. Down on the corner."

"He lives in a group home, doesn't he?"

"Yeah, he does." T.J. was afraid this might become one of those *how lucky he is to have you for a friend* conversations, so he asked Gaines what he wanted.

"I thought I'd ask you if you'd like to take a few notes at Full Court. Call me when you get back and maybe we can get a story out of it."

"Why?" asked T.J.

"Most of the best players in the state will be there, as well as several of the top prospects in the Midwest. A lot of high-profile college coaches will be there. If you kept your ears on, you might hear something."

"You mean like who's going to which college, right?"

"Sure."

He asked Gaines, "Why aren't you covering the camp yourself?"

"I would if I could, but there's an international softball tournament down in Belleville. I'll be there all week. I don't like it, but that's where my editor is sending me."

"I don't know. I'll keep my ears open, but I

won't promise about taking notes."

"Did I mention the paper would be willing to pay you?"

T.J. didn't know if this made it any better or any worse, but it certainly got his attention. "Let me think a minute," he said to the sportswriter. "I'll be right back." He went into the kitchen where he could be alone, where there might be some sanctuary for this *thinking* he needed to do.

It would be easy enough, for sure. All he would have to do would be to keep his ears open and then pass pieces of information about big-time players at the camp to a newspaper writer. But it didn't feel right, somehow. It reminded him too much of the diary he had been keeping for several months in which he made notes about Tyron's letters and contacts from college coaches.

He entered the bathroom and began scrubbing his face and hands. The diary really seemed lame at times, and it also seemed lame how important you suddenly were if you were the closest friend of a big-time college prospect.

Back in the kitchen, on top of the table clutter consisting of catalogs and third-class advertising circulars, was a note from his mother. In the freezer, according to the note, were eight pigs in a blanket wrapped in a box that used to house Tyson frozen chicken breasts. *Take these with you,* instructed his mother's looping cursive, *and they'll be thawed by suppertime.* T.J. couldn't help but smile. His mother couldn't get past the notion that *camp* meant they would be sleeping in lean-tos and fishing along the riverbank for food to eat.

The note had a P.S.: *As soon as you get back, I want you to show me some more stuff about the Quicken.* He had to smile again. Quicken was the financial program his mother was studying in a night school computer course. Sometimes explaining computer information to her was as challenging as interpreting scoring averages for Tyron.

He took the box of frozen pigs in a blanket, then gathered up his wallet and car keys. As soon as he was on the porch again he asked Gaines, "How much would the paper pay me?"

"Can't say for sure. We'd have to see what you find out."

"We'll see," said T.J. It wasn't the kind of

thing he could make up his mind about on a moment's notice. Tyron was approaching the driveway with his huge Georgetown duffel bag slung over his shoulder. He was wearing the headphones of his Discman.

Gaines was smiling. "I told you he was going to be good, didn't I?"

"Yeah, you did." said T.J.

"He scored twenty-two points a game and averaged double-figure rebounds. I told you he was a prospect, didn't I?"

"Yeah, you did."

They loaded the car and left. Tyron reclined the passenger's seat as far as it would go, but his knees still jammed up awkwardly against the dash. At six feet nine inches, and 270 pounds, the big guy wasn't likely to find a physical comfort zone in a small Japanese car. Tyron's open, ingenuous face was smooth-complexioned, the rich color of coffee with milk added. His too-long nappy hair constructed an out-of-date Afro shag, but it made a convenient resting place for his marbled pick.

"Do me a favor, Tyron," said T.J. "Take the pick out of your hair, okay?"

Tyron frowned. "But why?"

"It's one of those things that gets interpreted as some kind of gang shit. We don't need that at the camp."

"My pick is nothin' to do with gangs."

"You and I know that, but not everybody else does. Coaches and administrators, they think everything unusual is some kind of gang shit. You don't want to do anything to get Lindsey suspicious. Or any other coach, for that matter."

Tyron leaned forward to slip the earphones of his Discman into place. He was so huge that in this position he blocked out all the light from the passenger's side window. The secured pick stuck out at an acute angle like the armature on a coatrack. He spoke in the direction of his knees: "I got a letter from Georgetown. From John Thompson."

"I know. Remember, you showed it to me?" Tyron had received letters from so many colleges, T.J. would have lost track long ago were it not for the diary he maintained. T.J. had given up trying to explain to him that most of them were merely formal letters of introduction; they didn't necessarily indicate any serious interest.

"Slam-dunkin' Hoyas, man," murmured Tyron.

"Take the pick out, okay, Tyron? All you have to do is put it in your pocket."

He took the pick out, but the flourish with which he cranked up his Boys II Men CD was a high-profile act of defiance.

By the time they reached the edge of town, T.J. found himself brainstorming the pros and cons of Gaines's offer.

Thinking about the sportswriter, he remembered the first time he ever met him, that time when workouts started last fall. Gaines had shown up at a practice wearing an olive green corduroy suit that was loose and shapeless. He had taken a seat next to T.J. while the scrimmage was in progress. He seemed to clean his glasses a lot, and T.J. tried to remember if he'd ever seen a corduroy suit before.

When the sportswriter saw the ice pack and wrap on T.J.'s left ankle, he asked the nature of the injury.

"It's nothin'," T.J. had answered. "Coach DeFreese told me to sit a while."

"Oh, tough guy, huh?"

"No, it's nothin'." It really *was* nothing, and certainly not the first time he'd ever faked an injury or exaggerated the seriousness of one. T.J. knew how rapid his recovery would be, how fully restored to health he'd be by suppertime. But he wasn't about to say so to this sportswriter or to anyone else.

For a few minutes they sat quietly, watching the scrimmage pound back and forth. It hadn't taken long for Gaines to focus his attention on Tyron. "What do you know about him?" the writer had asked.

T.J. could have answered, *just about everything there is to know.* But instead, he had simply replied, "He's my friend. I know him."

"You're a transfer too, aren't you?"

"Yeah, I'm a transfer too."

"You transfer together?"

"No. He transferred this year. I transferred last year."

"You know a lot about him, then." By this time, Gaines had taken out a notebook and a ballpoint. "How'd he do as a sophomore?"

"You mean back in the city?"

"Yeah, how'd he do?"

T.J. took the time to adjust his wrap, but it was only a stalling tactic. He didn't know Gaines, so what should he tell him? A sportswriter was probably someone who could hurt you or help you, so you couldn't just blurt out any information that came to mind. "Why are you so interested in Bumpy?" he finally asked.

"Bumpy?"

"I mean Tyron. That's just an old nickname from when he was a kid; forget I even said it. But why are you so interested in him?"

"Well, he's a six-nine transfer from Chicago. It's not the kind of thing that happens every day, is it? I have to check him out."

T.J. was set to ponder these remarks, when Gaines continued. "Until he proves otherwise, I have to assume he's going to be an impact player."

"And?"

"Well," Gaines had said, while cleaning his glasses for the third or fourth time, "look at him."

T.J. watched. He could see how Tyron

looked a lot more like a good player now that so much of the baby fat was gone. He moved better too, probably for that very reason. One time down the floor, when Morgan beat his man along the baseline and jumped to try a finger roll, Tyron left his man to swat the shot off the end of the court.

Another time, on offense, getting his man on his hip posted up, he snatched a bad pass with his left hand, then turned in the lane to sink a soft jumper. "Look at that," pointed out Gaines. "Strong hands. He catches the ball with one hand while holding his position, then shows nice balance rolling into the lane."

"Yeah, I guess," said T.J. He didn't know much about Gaines, but the sportswriter's evident knowledge of basketball was urging him to look at Tyron with fresh eyes.

"That's the first thing a college scout looks for," Gaines had added.

College scout?? thought T.J., astonished. *Did he say college scout?* "Did you say something about college scouts?"

"Yeah. The first thing they look for, especially in a big man, is can he catch the ball? How are his hands? Can he post up strong and catch the ball in traffic?"

A college scout?

"Your friend's only a junior," Gaines had reminded him. "That's what to look for, strong hands in traffic. Keep it in mind when you watch him."

T.J. tried, but all he could keep in mind was Tyron's low IQ and even lower grades. He had to laugh, almost, it was so comical to think of Tyron and a college coach sitting down to have a meaningful conversation.

By the time the scrimmage had entered its last five minutes, Tyron's fatigue had taken over, so he was essentially the player T.J. was familiar with. He was lazy down the court, easily discouraged by missed shots or turnovers. He was only a factor if the game was strictly in the half-court mode, and even then only a marginal one. T.J. wondered if Gaines saw those things too, or only the stuff that might make good newspaper reading. College scouts? He had to give credit where credit was due, though; without Gaines's input, he never would have appreciated Tyron's potential.

T.J. put the scrimmage memory aside and returned to the present. By the time they were south of Springfield, he began to watch for exit signs while he kept an intermittent eye on the temperature gauge. The old Toyota was hinky in half a dozen ways, but most especially in the department of overheating.

Tyron kept shifting uncomfortably in the passenger's seat, struggling to find a way to conform his huge bulk to the inadequate available space. Finally, he gave it up: "T.J., can we stop somewhere? I have to piss."

T.J. was lighting a cigarette. "We've only got about six miles to go, once we get off the highway. Can't you wait?"

"I have to piss real bad."

"Okay, we'll stop."

TWO

THEY stopped at a roadhouse only a mile or two off the interstate. Standing at a rural crossroads, it bore the name of HEAVEN'S GATE in white painted letters on green shingle siding. The way the white gravel in the parking lot reflected the heat of the blazing sun, T.J. had to think a name with *hell* in it would have been more appropriate. There was nothing heavenly once you got inside, either. Heaven's Gate was a combination redneck bar, convenience store, tacky grocery store, and sit-down restaurant.

There were lop-eared girlie magazines and supermarket tabloids next to the cash register, and a homemade sign by the beer corner said, WE CARD EVERYBODY; IF YOU WANT BREW, HAVE

YOUR I.D. READY. A narrow wing with poor lighting and restaurant-style tables wrapped around the bar. There was loud laughing from some of the men seated there drinking beer and playing cards. Some of the faces were familiar to T.J.; he recognized them as coaches, even if he couldn't recall their names. He decided they must be here to watch players at Full Court, and this would be their watering hole.

Before they left the roadhouse, Tyron bought a large bag of potato chips and a sixteen-ounce bottle of Mountain Dew. T.J. drove tentatively while Tyron gobbled on his chips. The primitive blacktop road he navigated slowly was characterized by twists and turns and sudden hills. The dense timber stood so near the shoulder that any view of the huge reservoir to their right came in the form of a brief glimpse every now and then across a small clearing. T.J. had to watch the rustic directional signs closely to avoid turning down the lanes that led to boat launches or other recreational areas.

It might have been an area of pastoral

beauty—in fact, probably was—but for T.J. it was too unfamiliar to be comfortable. Besides the fact he'd never been here before, it was too woodsy. There was a severe absence of pavement. This was the *forest*. T.J. had spent all but the past two years of his life on the streets of Chicago. Heaven's Gate, it seemed to him, stood at the threshold of a remote and doubtful region of daunting wilderness, much more purgatory than paradise.

These thoughts made a cloud in his brain, but then Tyron intruded: "What's in the box, T.J.?"

"What box?"

"In the backseat, that chicken box."

"Oh. Those are pigs in a blanket. My mother made 'em."

"What's pigs in a blanket?"

"Hot dogs. They're baked in crescent rolls."

"Can I have one?" Tyron asked.

"You can have all you want, but they're probably not thawed yet. What about the potato chips?"

"I want somethin' else. I'm still hungry."

"Have all you want," T.J. said, motioning.

Tyron had four, crunching them like candy bars, all the while extolling their virtue with his mouth full.

The Full Court campers got to stay in the conference center part of the complex. It was a package of creature comforts far beyond what T.J. expected; it was even air-conditioned. They were housed three to a room, and each room had its own bathroom. Downstairs, in addition to the cafeteria, was a large conference room and a rec room with big-screen TV and several video games.

When T.J. and Tyron unpacked their stuff, T.J.'s only dilemma was where he should put his diary. It was the only thing in his possession that demanded privacy. He finally decided to take it back to the parking lot, where he could leave it in the glove box. Keep the car locked.

They met their roommate, a player from Peoria named Obie Williams. They had played against him junior year, but they hadn't ever talked to him. Obie wasn't bashful. He asked T.J., "What color are you, anyway?"

It was a question T.J. got asked frequently. He smiled before he answered, "Sort of light brown; beige, you might say."

"Say what?"

"Color. You know, color?"

"I'm askin' you what color are you?" Obie persisted.

"I'm tryin' to answer. My father was Italian, and my mother is Puerto Rican. Actually, she's not Puerto Rican, but her parents were. You could say she's Puerto Rican, except she's never been there. She's never been out of Illinois, I don't think."

"That ain't no kind of answer, I'm askin' are you black or are you white?"

"It's the best answer I've got. I'm a hybrid, sort of."

This wasn't going to satisfy the perplexed roommate either. "What's a hybrid?" Obie wanted to know.

"It's okay, you can call me bro if you want."

"Say what?"

The high school coaches and college students

who stayed in first-floor rooms were in charge of the building—they were the chaperones, more or less. There was a lot of commotion because there were more than two hundred players moved in or moving in. T.J. felt like he was the only one who didn't have a Discman.

In the cafeteria, a schedule was posted; it informed them there would be an orientation meeting at 3:30. Once he discovered the video games in the rec room, Tyron was mellowed to the max. He couldn't have been more at home even back at home. T.J., though, took off on his own. He felt the need to conduct a more personal, private orientation, one that could establish his sense of place.

He found his way to the parking lot, where he secured the diary in the car. He walked along the footpath that led in the direction of the huge footbridge in the distance. He passed six tartan-surfaced basketball courts where they would be playing their games; coaches and officials were setting up water tables between the courts, along with folding chairs. Shortly after, he passed the swimming pool, which was full of younger children squealing and hollering. He wondered briefly if Full Court campers would get to use the pool.

When he reached the footbridge, he saw how large it was, and how crude. It reached a distance of some two hundred feet or more from the bluff where he was standing to the bluff on the other side. It was put together with telephone poles and rough planks, but it looked very sturdy.

T.J. was standing on the high ground, where he could see. It felt reassuring to stand here; every army commander who ever lived, he knew from reading military history, proclaimed the advantage of the high ground. Looking back and to the right, he could see the facilities he had passed shortly before, even the conference center where they were staying. Looking across to the other side, he could see clusters of buildings in the distance, big ones and small ones. He realized there were more people and organizations here than Full Court could account for.

Reconnaissance had always been crucial to T.J. Nucci. You had to know the dimensions of the system within which you were supposed to function. You had to know the boundaries and the limits, as well as the gaps that created opportunities. In order to establish control of situations, you had to have bearings. And bearings were based on information.

Even when he was as young as twelve, he had learned the surveillance habit of sniffing out potential danger posed by his stepfather (*ex*-stepfather, actually). It wasn't unusual for Lloyd to break the terms of the judge's protection order by returning to their apartment to harass T.J.'s mother. Usually before he even turned the corner on their block, T.J. had learned to be alert for details. Was the Cougar parked along the curb near their building? If not, were there any cars he didn't recognize? Any police cars? When he got closer, he would look for beer cans or wine bottles on the stoop. If he saw any, what kind were they? If it was after dark, he looked to see which lights were on, or listened for pitched voices.

The bridge smelled strongly of the creosote used to weatherize it. T.J. lit a cigarette as he started to cross it. It was a long way down to the bottom of the gorge, where a nearly dry creek bed gurgled, barely, in some rocky shallows. With no breeze, it smelled brackish. On the other side he discovered, among other things, a group of shop and equipment buildings where maintenance workers were hanging out. Several of them were seated at a pair of picnic tables beneath a huge oak tree, drinking coffee and telling jokes. It brought back the unpleasant memory of last summer's job, when he had been on a weed-cutting crew out at the reservoir.

He got back to the conference center in time to participate in the team selections, which were made along regional lines. He and Tyron were on the same team, which was the thing he cared about most. Ishmael Greene, a superstar by reputation, was also selected for their team. So was Obie, their roommate. Each team had a total of ten players. T.J. could only hope the rest of his teammates were guys who could play, or else he would be expected to play more minutes than he wanted.

When it was time to name the team, Tyron suggested they should be called the Blue Stars. T.J. recognized it as a space ranger group from some SEGA game, but it turned out to be a popular suggestion. The Blue Stars they would be, and the positive reinforcement of receiving early approval could only be beneficial to Tyron at the camp.

Their first game wasn't until after supper when the heat was down, but it was still too warm to go full out, as far as T.J. was concerned. He was in over his head here, anyway; if it hadn't been for the need to ride herd on Bumpy and keep him encouraged, he wouldn't have been here at all.

It didn't take more than five or six minutes of the first half for T.J. to realize how overmatched he was by these other players. These guys were essentially all-stars, the elite players on their high school teams. They were showcasing their skills for the benefit of the many college recruiters on hand.

On his own team, in addition to Tyron, Ishmael Greene demonstrated in a hurry why he was rated among the best players in the state. Ishmael was an incredible leaper with amazing skills; it was nearly impossible to guard him because he was also a deadly shooter from the perimeter. It was rumored he was leaning toward Notre Dame, but the rumor didn't stop the multitude of other coaches from hovering close to the court. In any case, it was a welcome benefit to T.J. having him on the team, because all you really had to do on offense was get the ball in Ishmael's hands and then relax.

Tyron was playing extremely well; the atmosphere of big-time teammates and college recruiters seemed to inspire him. In the second half, T.J. welcomed the opportunity to sit on the bench while other guys played. It wasn't appropriate that he was chosen to be in the starting lineup, anyway; he wasn't even a starter for his high school team. Not that he wanted to be.

From the bench, he watched the activity around the courts more than the game itself. In addition to all the college coaches and recruiters, there were a number of other guys he didn't recognize, some young and some not so young. Some of them must have been coaches he didn't know about, but they couldn't all be; there were too many of them. A lot of them wore caps from pro teams like the Magic or the Hornets. Others wore shorts and shirts with Nike logos or Adidas symbols. T.J. guessed they were friends and relatives of players, or other players not signed up for the camp.

Once, when Ishmael Greene went out of the game to take a breather, T.J. saw the Notre Dame coach have a brief conversation with him. T.J. knew, from his conversations with Coach Lindsey at North State, that such a conversation was illegal. It was a violation of NCAA rules. College coaches were allowed to be present at Full Court and watch the players for purposes of evaluation, but the rules said they couldn't make contact. T.J. wondered if he should write it down in his diary, but then he remembered it had nothing to do with Tyron, so what would be the point? But it would be exactly the kind of thing the sportswriter Gaines would want to hear about. T.J. had to giggle, in spite of himself; was this supposed to be basketball, or espionage?

Other teams played at eight o'clock, so they got to rest for an hour before their second game, which was under the lights. It was somewhat cooler after sundown, but not nearly enough to satisfy T.J. For some reason, the coach started him again. He was expected to try and check a jet-quick guard from Chicago named Ronnie Streets. It was hopeless. In addition to his fatigue, T.J. was annoyed. If he had fully realized the level of talent he would be expected to compete against, and the intensity of physical exertion involved, he would have stayed at home and let Tyron fend for himself.

After about six minutes or so, he turned his ankle trying to chase Streets down the lane. It was only a mild turn; T.J. knew it was far removed from an actual injury like a sprain, but he was grateful for any chance to lie on his back and look up at the stars.

"You okay, Nucci?" It was their coach, Buddy Ingalls, asking him. Ingalls was actually a player from Bradley.

"It's my ankle," T.J. replied.

The coach fingered his ankle. "Is it bad?"

"I can't say yet."

"Do you need to see one of the trainers?"

T.J. was disappointed in himself for not

thinking of it sooner than his coach did. The
trainers were good-looking college babes, and
their building was air conditioned. "Maybe I
ought to," he said, "just to be safe." He
wasn't proud of the fraud, but sometimes
duplicity was the only option you had.

Both of the trainers in Room A were blondes
with dark tans, Southern Illinois University students majoring in leisure studies or sports
medicine. The one named Nola removed his
left shoe and sock, while the one named Bridget
was working a crossword puzzle. The room
itself was big-time cool, and the table he lay on
was cool vinyl. When Nola probed his ankle
with her fingers, T.J. felt very little pain. He
could only hope there might be at least a little
swelling to make this encounter seem legiti-
mate.

"I can't find any swelling," said Nola flatly,
"but I'll ice it for you, anyway. You can probably play the second half of your game if you
feel up to it."

"Thanks. We'll see." There was nothing to
see, though. The ice pack would be as com-
pelling as a written pass from the dean's office.

Nola was applying the Freezepack and using an Ace bandage wrap to secure it around the ankle. Looking up from her puzzle book, Bridget asked, "Have you ever heard of a word called *feckless*?"

"Called what?" asked Nola.

"Feckless. Have you ever heard of it?"

"No. Why?"

"Well, it fits in here. It fits in eighteen across."

"I never heard of any word like that. You must have a mistake in there someplace."

"I don't think so," Bridget insisted. "I think all the other words are right."

Now that Nola was finished with his ankle wrap, T.J. was free to turn onto his side. He had never heard of *feckless* before either. "It sounds like it might be a real word," he said, "But there would be a problem with it."

"What problem?"

"Well, think about it. A word with *less* on the end means you don't have any of something. In this case, it would have to mean you don't have any *feck*."

"But what is feck?" Bridget asked him.

"Exactly. What does it mean to have no feck? What does it mean to *have* feck? I mean, compare it to a word like *helpless* or *painless*. You see where this is headed?"

She was trying not to giggle. "More or less."

"So the problem would be, if you don't have any feck, what is it that you're missing? Is it a good thing to have, or a bad thing?"

"Are we done now?" asked Nola, with an officious tone of voice.

T.J. ignored her by asking, "Is feck something you're born with or is it something you acquire? Are there people with lots of feck only they don't know it? Is there like a standard range for it, like you could be hyperfeck or hypofeck?"

Bridget was laughing out loud, but Nola wasn't finding anything amusing about T.J.'s malingering. "I think we're done here," she declared.

"Okay, okay." T.J. swung himself into the seated position on the edge of the table. The ankle wrap felt secure. Still in a playful head, he asked Nola, "Are you busy later tonight?"

"Too busy to baby-sit," she replied, without missing a beat.

"Ouch. Maybe you'd like to think it over."

"I'm sure."

When he was courtside again, he found Tyron sitting on the bench. He had taken himself out of the game.

"Why?" asked T.J.

"I'm so goddam tired, T.J. Let's go back to the rec room and play those video games."

"When?"

"Now. Let's go now."

T.J. was flabbergasted. "We can't go now! We can't just leave in the middle of a game!"

"But I'm so goddam tired." Tyron was quaffing Gatorade in huge cups, one after the other, while the sweat poured down his face.

And this is only the first day, T.J. reminded himself. "We can play video games later tonight. No pain, no gain, Big Guy. Remember, if you want to be a star, you have to pay the price."

"Maybe I don't want to be a star."

"What about the slam-dunkin' Hawkeyes and the slam-dunkin' Hoyas?"

"But maybe I don't want to be a star. Maybe I want to spend my time at the mall, hangin' out."

"Are you crazy? Look at me, I'm the one with the injury, but do you hear me talkin' about quittin'?"

Now Tyron was ashamed. "No," he said.

T.J. pushed the advantage: "Even with this ankle, do you hear me say anything about quitting? Do you?"

"I said no, didn't I?"

"Then take five and go back in. What will Coach Lindsey think if he sees you bein' lame like this?"

"Okay, okay."

THREE

THEY had two games the next morning. Since it wasn't the hottest part of the day, T.J. played as much as he was asked. The ankle wasn't hurting him; if it needed to be a factor somehow, he could wait until the temperature got up to ninety degrees or higher.

Tyron was playing extremely well. So well, in fact, that at times he seemed to dominate, at least on the inside. He was also wearing a brand-new pair of shoes, some top-of-the-line Nikes that T.J. didn't recognize. When there was a break between games, he asked Tyron about the shoes.

"Bee Edwards gave them to me," replied Tyron. He was short of breath, but smiling.

"Who's Bee Edwards, and why did he give

you shoes?" T.J. was looking closely. They were the Nike Magic Carpets, with the distinct amber bubble nestled in the crook of the *swoosh*. "You know how much these shoes cost?"

It was too many questions at one time for Tyron, whose confusion was apparent.

"Okay," said T.J. "Who's Bee Edwards? Tell me that."

"He's just a guy. I don't know who he is."

T.J. thought he might know the man to whom Tyron was referring. "Not the guy with the hat. You don't mean the guy with the hat."

"Yeah, that's the guy. He gave me the shoes."

"*Why* did he give you the shoes?"

Tyron was toweling off his face. "You could slow down with the questions, right?"

"Why did he give you the shoes?"

"He gave Ishmael a pair of shoes, and I said I'd like to have some too."

"So he gave them to you? Just like that?"

"Yeah."

"Jesus Christ," said T.J. He turned to Ishmael Greene and asked, "That's the way it happened, he gave you a pair of shoes, so then he gives Bumpy a pair too?"

"Who's Bumpy?"

"I meant Tyron. Is that how it happened?"

"That's how it happened, man. Bee gave me a pair, then he gave Tyron a pair. It's no big deal. He gives me shoes from time to time, but he's not the only one. Know what I mean?"

"I don't have a clue what you mean," T.J. answered. But for the exasperation he was feeling, he might have taken the time to write some of this stuff down for Gaines, the sportswriter. He dismissed the thought as fast as it came. "What are you supposed to do for the shoes?" he asked Ishmael.

"Do?" said Ishmael. "Say *do*? Don't do shit, man. *Nada*."

T.J. really did want to get a handle on this, even though he was already tired of hearing about it. "Bee Edwards gives you shoes. Then he gives other people shoes. In return, he expects nothing for it."

"That's it. I think he used to hope I'd go to Kentucky, but that's not it anymore. I think it's just that he likes me."

"Why would he care if you go to Kentucky? Never mind, don't answer that."

Their coach for the week, Buddy Ingalls, who stood only about five eleven, was a varsity guard for Bradley. He was a noisy, scrappy type; T.J. recognized him as the kind of player who was usually called a *spark plug*. Ingalls told them to shut up so he could give them their second-game strategy. But he had heard enough of the conversation to warn, "Street agents, man. Fucking hustlers. Keep away from them."

Then Buddy began talking about zones and traps, but T.J. wasn't listening. He thought to himself, *This is just great. I'm in over my head on the court, and Tyron is in over his head off the court.*

Lunch was good, but the food was always good. Besides the salad bar and the dessert bar, there were enough barbecue sandwiches for seconds and even thirds. T.J. was sure they were all getting their money's worth, but nobody more so than Tyron. The place would probably go broke if they had to feed him over the long haul.

He could see coaches coming and going from their dining area, which was in a private room. It was one more procedure designed to keep them separate from players, so they wouldn't make contact. While he was eating his dessert, T.J. read the front section of the *Chicago Tribune*. When he saw Coach Lindsey from North State he waved, and Lindsey waved back. Seeing Lindsey caused him to think of Bee Edwards and the shoes, although it didn't seem likely that the one thing would have anything to do with the other.

After lunch, Ingalls told them to get plenty of rest because the first game of the afternoon was against the Chicago team, a team they would have to beat to get in the championship round of the tournament. Then Tyron headed straight for the video games, while T.J. went up to their room.

Obie Williams, their roommate, was already there, taking a nap. He was snoring away. T.J. lay on his back with his hands behind his head. He wanted a chance to talk to Coach Lindsey before the week was out, but it was against the rules. It might happen anyway, though.

Because of Obie's snoring, T.J. knew he wouldn't be going to sleep, but he felt mellow enough to take a trip down memory lane, back to that night last season when he had talked to Lindsey for the first time.

It was right after the Champaign game. "We're very interested in Tyron," Lindsey had said, "as I'm sure you know. We think you might be in a position to help us."

"How would I do that?"

"Well, just having you in our corner would be the biggest help, of course. Besides that, we'd like to ask if you might be willing to keep a journal or a diary."

"What diary?"

Lindsey had continued by saying, "If you'd be willing to keep a written log of who calls him, who visits him at home, who comes to watch him play. That sort of thing."

"You're talkin' about coaches, right?"

"Mostly coaches, yes. But anyone else who might show an interest in him as well. You'd be surprised at what kinds of characters can surface in this business. We'd also like to know which schools appeal to him, and why. In recruiting, it's always an advantage to have information."

T.J. didn't have to be convinced of the value of information, but he was already wondering to himself, *what would be in it for me*? This was a conversation where he would have to watch his step, so he had asked Lindsey, "If you want to recruit Tyron, why don't you talk to Coach DeFreese?"

"We already have and we'll continue to talk to him. But we also know you have influence with Tyron. He trusts you. We believe he would listen to your advice in connection with any major decision he might need to make."

"How do you know so much about me 'n' Tyron?"

Coach Lindsey had smiled before crossing his leg. "I already told you: Information is vital to the recruiting process."

Lindsey was a slick guy, which was as obvious from his personal appearance as from the way he talked. A pale blue collar, starched and crisp, emerged from the V of his maroon North State sweater. His shoes were ultra shiny like patent leather; maybe they *were* patent leather. But if slick was slick, then fair was fair; since this coach was asking him for a favor, and a big favor at that, he decided to find out if there was a next level. "Would there be anything in this for me?"

Lindsey's chuckle was the prelude to his answer. "We wouldn't ask you to do this for nothing, would we?"

"So what are we talkin' about?"

"You want a dollar amount? Is that what you're asking me?"

T.J. wasn't sure what his answer should be, but it seemed like this was another level, still. He retreated: "Do you have any idea how dumb Tyron is? What kind of a student he is?"

"We do indeed."

"And that doesn't bother you? I mean, we're talkin' about a guy who's in over his head in Phase Three English. I don't get it."

But Lindsey had replied, "We have a strategy for qualifying marginal students. It's called 504."

"504?"

"Public Law 504 changes everything."

"How does it change everything?" T.J. had asked. "What is it?"

"It's a public education law that allows students to be rediagnosed. It allows a student who hasn't done well in school to be classified as a student with a disability."

T.J. wondered what would be good about being classified as disabled. But he wanted to hear more. "I don't get the point," he admitted to the coach.

"If Tyron could somehow qualify as a learning disabled student, it would give him some leeway with standardized testing such as the SAT or the ACT."

"What leeway?"

"He would be permitted to have the test read to him. The usual test advocate is a special education teacher or a school counselor."

T.J. remembered when he had taken the ACT; it was a test to bust your balls. He couldn't imagine Tyron even taking the test, let alone getting a decent score. Then he tried to imagine him taking it if someone read it to him. "That would be an advantage, wouldn't it?"

"It's a huge advantage," Lindsey had concurred immediately. "Especially since he could take it without a time limit."

"No time limit?"

"None. He could take it a couple hours a day, spread out over a week or two if he wanted. Did you take the ACT?"

"Yeah."

"Then I don't have to tell you how much easier it would be to get a passing score if you could work with no time limit."

T.J.'s head was spinning with data and possibilities. "Why are you telling me all of this?" he had asked. "*I* can't read him the test, can I?"

"No, but you're a resourceful young man. Information, T.J. Just remember: *information*. You're his friend and you want to help him."

It was the part they *weren't* mentioning, though, the dollar figures. But T.J. was clever enough to know it would be to his advantage to let the North State people name the amount. "Okay," he had asked, "how do you get to be 504?"

Coach Lindsey had used a Chap Stick on the corners of his mouth before answering. "It takes an advocate. Someone who understands that students aren't necessarily dumb or lazy just because their academic performance is weak. They may be fighting a learning disability that nobody knows about because they slipped through the cracks."

"What cracks?"

"It usually means that their disability was overlooked somehow or missed by school authorities. Tyron received most of his education in the Chicago public schools; so did you. I don't need to tell you how many cracks there are in that system."

It sort of drew T.J. up in the pit of his stomach to understand that he was in a position to bargain with a major college coach. On anything. He had taken a deep breath before he repeated, "Because I'm his friend."

"Because you're his *main man*; because you want to help him." The coach was smiling.

It had been at this point in the conversation when Tyron approached, so they had gone their separate ways. On the drive home, Tyron had asked right away what Coach Lindsey had to say.

"You had twenty points, Tyron. He was impressed."

"Not bad, huh?"

"Not bad at all. Like I say, Lindsey was impressed."

"Jesus." Tyron tried to stretch, but the car was too small. "So is twenty my average now?"

"Your average isn't the same as the points you got in your last game."

"*Tonight* is my last game. I got twenty."

T.J. let out a sigh before he had tried once more to explain the concept of a scoring average. Tyron listened briefly, but grew impatient. "Tell me what Coach Lindsey said."

By this time they were in T.J.'s driveway. It was too cold to turn off the engine, so he left it idling. The bedroom lamp was on, which meant his mother was home. "Coach Lindsey says you have Division One potential."

"Jesus."

"Do you have to say *Jesus* all the time, Bumpy? It gets like tiresome, you know what I mean?"

"Okay, but don't call me Bumpy."

"Sorry. Coach Lindsey also says you're a project. You have to remember that."

"Okay, but I don't know what it means."

"It means you're not ready yet. I showed

you the column Gaines wrote. You remember, I cut it out for you?"

"I remember how complicated it was."

"Let's boil it down. If you're a project, that means you have a lot of work to do. You could be a great player if you worked hard at getting in shape, spending time in the weight room, improving your grades, et cetera et cetera."

"Yeah, but don't forget the payoff," Tyron had reminded him, with his head down. The thought of hard work was always discouraging.

T.J. had sighed again while he cut off the engine. He was pretty good at avoiding the pitfall of physical fatigue, but befriending Tyron was an ongoing invitation to mental fatigue. He glanced sidelong at his mountainous *compadre*. Could block out the streetlight or the moonlight just as well as the sun, but trying to imagine him as a college basketball star, as a *student/athlete*, that seemed more far-fetched than a thing should be.

Nevertheless, hadn't Lindsey outlined for him the 504 concept? A coach at North State ought to know what he was talking about. T.J. said to Tyron, "The payoff is glory."

"Glory." Tyron repeated the word reverently.

Tell me about the rabbits, George. Tell me about the part where I get to tend the rabbits, T.J. thought to himself. But he said, "Playing in places like Pauley Pavilion and Madison Square Garden. Playing on ESPN and CBS. Flying in jet planes all over the country and staying in fancy hotels. You get the picture, don't make me say it again."

"Jesus."

By this time T.J. had been too tired to continue the conversation; besides, it was getting cold in the car. "I'm goin' to bed," he declared. "You better go on home before you miss your curfew."

"Don't remind me about curfew. Curfew is a thing I hate."

"Do me a favor, Tyron?"

"What favor?"

"Turn your hat around."

The thing that woke him up was Obie Williams shaking him by the arm. "Let's go, Nucci," Obie was saying. "Ingalls says we only got twenty minutes."

The next game, T.J. thought to himself. His stroll down memory lane had put him to sleep. He swung himself into the seated position on the edge of the bed and started rubbing his eyes. "You know what, Obie? You snore like a chain saw."

"Is that it? You ready or what?"

"I'm ready, I'm ready."

When they left the air-conditioned dorm, though, and walked into the teeth of the two P.M. heat, T.J. wondered if he really was ready. It was a distinct possibility that his ankle might be giving him trouble by the second game, if not by the second half of the first game.

The Blue Stars kept winning. Besides the incomparable Ishmael, Obie Williams was a good player, and Tyron was playing as well as T.J. had ever seen him. Once, when T.J. and Ishmael were sitting out at the same time, T.J. said it was amazing that Tyron wasn't worn out and discouraged.

Ishmael grinned at him. "Must be the shoes, man."

T.J. had to laugh. "Must be."

"Got to be the shoes, man."

When T.J. entered the game, he had to endure the task of guarding Streets again. It was hopeless. Streets was tireless, quick, and strong. There was an upside to T.J.'s situation, though; Ingalls had figured out by now that he was one of the lesser players on the team, so he played him fewer minutes. Maybe a sore ankle gambit wouldn't be necessary.

Between games, T.J. mopped his sweat and drank a whole bottle of Gatorade. Buddy Ingalls was telling them, "If they're going to play that zone, you have to punish them for it. A zone is a cop-out; make them pay the price." T.J. could tell what kind of coach Buddy would be one day. He would be one of those roosters with a flower in his lapel, prowling the sidelines with a steady chatter and a cock-of-the-roost sort of strut.

He tuned Buddy out so he could observe the crowd of adults hovering near the courts, the coaches, the assistant coaches, and the groupies. Even they were hot, wiping sweat and drinking Pepsis. T.J. picked out Bee Edwards talking to a coach from Purdue. He was wearing a hat that looked like an under-sized cowboy hat, but it had the Nike logo on it. Every garment he wore had the Nike logo, even his socks.

He's a street agent, Ingalls had said. *A hustler.* T.J. remembered Coach Lindsey's words too: *You'd be surprised at what kinds of characters can surface in this business.*

When the second game started, T.J. made sure he was sitting next to Buddy Ingalls. He asked him what a street agent was.

"A douche bag," said Ingalls.

"Yeah, but what does he do?"

"Anything he can to score something with a prospect. He's into a power trip."

"You mean like giving them shoes?"

"Yeah, like shoes, or sweats, or drugs, or helpin' out a family member. It's usually the kind of player who doesn't have parents to guide him, or a coach who's not heavy into the recruiting process. The street agent is lookin' to be the middle man. That way, all the coaches and recruiters will have to go through him."

For a moment, T.J. was uncomfortably aware that Buddy might have been describing

Tyron, or even—God forbid—himself. The
naivete he felt was equally uncomfortable
because it was the feeling of being in over your
head. When you were in over your head, that
was when you became a victim. Nevertheless,
he asked Buddy, "So what about Bee
Edwards?"

"Yeah, he's one of 'em."

"Does he, like, work for Nike, though?"

"He will work for them if he thinks it'll get
him ahead. He'll work for anybody as long as
it puts him where he wants to be. Street agents
work for themselves, that's the bottom line."

T.J. knew he needed more information if he
expected to really be in touch with this
unwholesome plane. And it was obviously
important. But he could tell from Buddy's tone
of voice that he wanted to concentrate on the
game itself instead of having more conversations about street agents. It was time to drop
the subject.

FOUR

THERE were no games that night. Instead, they were having a film and a motivational speaker. The speaker was Digger Phelps, the former Notre Dame coach and current TV broadcaster, but T.J. had no enthusiasm for a bunch of rah-rah about staying in school, doing your homework, and keeping away from drugs. He'd never been a user in his life and as for schoolwork, he was already an A/B student.

He escaped to the footbridge where he could be alone. Every muscle in his body was stiff from so many basketball games. He let his feet swing over the edge. He smoked a cigarette while he watched the sun go down, and then he lit up another one. It was so quiet he could hear the singing and shouting from the bluff on the far side. He had heard there was a Holy Roller camp over there, but he didn't know much about it.

When it was dusk, he could barely make out the gorge below, but he could sure make out the smell; there wasn't enough water in the creek bed to flush it with movement. T.J. wondered briefly if he was brave enough to stay here until after dark before making his way back to the dorm. Most of the players at the Full Court camp, because of their prevailing urban origins, were afraid to be out alone after dark amid the timber that covered the bluffs. The *forest dark* was what Ishmael called it. Tyron referred to it as the *darkest dark*.

It made T.J. uneasy too. If he had a higher level of courage than his fellow campers, it was probably owing to the reconnaissance he'd conducted when they first arrived. He knew the lay of the land a little better than most of the others. This fact, along with the faint but functional pole lights that were positioned occasionally along the walking trails, provided him with enough orientation for nighttime confidence.

He was in the process of reconstructing the conversations he'd had about Tyron's new pair of Nike Magic Carpets when a girl approached. She came from his left. If she had been sitting nearby, he hadn't noticed. "Can you take out splinters?" she asked.

T.J. was startled; he asked her to say it again.

"Do you know anything about taking out splinters? I think I've got one in my arm here where I can't see it." She seemed very unself-conscious as she sat down beside him. She was wearing a short, midriff T-shirt without sleeves and a pair of cutoff blue jeans. She lifted her right arm to show him the back side of her bicep. "See?"

When T.J. looked, he could see that the splinter was easily an inch and a half long; three fourths of it was under the skin. "This is big. How did you get this?"

"Is it big? I was laying my arms over the railing."

"You can't do that, though. The wood is too rough." T.J. took her right elbow and lifted it so the upper arm was horizontal. With the fingers of his left hand, he yanked out the splinter. The quicker the better, he figured.

Instead of complaining about any pain, she giggled. "Thank you," she said.

Even in the trailing light, he could see that her short hair was sort of a burgundy color, but it looked sloppy. "It was good for me," he said. "Was it good for you too?"

She laughed. "I'm sure the Lord will bless you for it."

He wouldn't try and figure that remark out, but it did tell him the girl was one of the ones from the Holy Roller camp. A small silver cross hung from the ring that pierced her belly button. He wondered briefly why a girl with metal through her navel would care about a wood sliver in her arm. He said to her, "Now that I've saved your life, maybe I ought to find out what your name is."

She paused before she answered. "LuAnn," she told him. "What's yours?"

"T.J. Nucci."

She asked him if he was in the basketball camp. It seemed to T.J. like she never stopped smiling.

"Yeah. Why?"

"Sometimes I can see across. There's a high place just outside our meeting shelter where you can see a long way. I can't see every court and every player, but some of it. Whenever I see the players, I think how hot it must be."

"Hotter 'n hell," T.J. agreed.

LuAnn giggled again. "I doubt that. I'm sure the fires of Hell are much hotter than anything we could ever imagine. You must be a real good player if you're in the Full Court camp."

"You know about basketball?"

"I used to be a cheerleader. Besides, everybody knows about Full Court."

"I wouldn't say *everybody*."

"You're probably right. Just people with an interest in basketball. You must be real good if you're in it, though."

"Not really." Briefly, and without going into too much detail, T.J. explained his relationship to Tyron. How he was here basically to keep Tyron motivated so he might get a college scholarship if the opportunity ever presented itself.

LuAnn listened with wide eyes. "I'm sure the Lord will bless you for it."

"Do you have to keep saying that? And how come you smile all the time?"

"I smile because I'm happy. I smile because I'm saved."

T.J. groaned in his mind, *Oh God.* The enthusiasm he'd been cultivating for her tits and legs fizzled like a doused charcoal briquette. *I suppose she's going to try to convert me.*

"Sister Simone teaches us that we can serve Him in all things, no matter how great or small."

"Who's Sister Simone?" asked T.J. Not that he really wanted to know.

"She's our counselor. She teaches us that all our problems, even the ones that seem most serious, can really be opportunities to glorify the Lord. But we have to seek His will and put our trust in Him."

And does she ever tell you to use your own brain for thinking? T.J. wondered. For the briefest moment, maybe no longer than a split second, when she spoke of Sister Simone he was reminded of Bee Edwards. *Why, though?* The thing he was sure about was that he didn't want to listen to a sermon about how he ought to turn his life over to the Lord. Wasn't he sitting on this bridge specifically to avoid Digger Phelps' sermonizing?

He couldn't tell for certain why he didn't leave at that point. It would be the easiest way. Instead, he took out a cigarette and lit it. When he offered her one, she said, "No, thank you."

"I don't suppose that would work with Sister Simone, would it?"

LuAnn was smiling. "It wouldn't work with me. It wouldn't work with who I am. It would only work with the old me."

"The old you?"

"Before I was saved. Before I turned my life over to the Lord. I used to smoke those things."

"You used to smoke and you used to be a cheerleader."

Her face was propped on her forearms, which were propped on the lower railing of the bridge. He liked her face at this three-quarter angle. She said, "I used to be a lot of things. Mostly, I was willful."

T.J. took a drag before he asked, "What's that supposed to mean, *willful*?"

"It means I wanted my own way. I had to be a cheerleader with a spiral perm. I smoked cigarettes and drank beer. I did some marijuana at parties. I skipped a lot of school, so my grades were low."

"What school do you go to?"

"Peoria Roosevelt. I'll be a senior next year."

"Yeah, me too. At Burton. So what happened to the cheerleading?"

"I was kicked off the squad."

"That's too bad," said T.J.

"Not really," LuAnn explained. "I think it's what I wanted. I wanted my parents to suffer. I thought all the bad things I was doing would punish them. It was so stupid how I was willing to mess up my own life just to pay them back for something I couldn't even name. That's what I mean by willful."

T.J., who was habitually guarded with the private aspects of his own life, wondered why LuAnn would be so open with all this negative personal history. "Do you always just blurt out the personal stuff?" he asked.

"I do now."

"Why?"

"Because telling other people I'm a sinner reminds me of the fact."

"You want to be reminded you're a sinner, is that it?" T.J. had no idea why he was even extending this conversation. He threw the spent Marlboro down the gorge.

"If you know you're a sinner," declared LuAnn, "it reminds you that you can be redeemed."

"So if you're bad, that's good."

She lifted her head to say, "If you acknowledge your sins and confess them, then God's grace can save you. If you don't understand your own sinful nature, then you can't understand the path to redemption."

"So you can't be saved if you don't admit you need it."

"Exactly." LuAnn smiled wider.

"Have you ever read *1984*?" T.J. asked her.

"I'm not sure," she replied. "Why?"

"Oh, you know, war is peace. Freedom is slavery."

"That sounds weird, for sure. Is it a good book?"

Now she sounded a little bit like Tyron, but

it didn't matter. Looking straight into her face, he wondered what he ought to say next. About all he could want from this girl was a good lay, but what he'd most likely get would be a session of scripture reading.

"I asked you, is it a good book?"

"Yeah," answered T.J., with no thought about books. "Lots of people think so."

"Are you a Christian, T.J.?" was her next question.

"No, no, nothin' like that," was his quick reply.

"Because our meetings are open. I'm sure Sister Simone would be glad to have you, or any of your friends."

"Do you think I need to be converted, is that it?"

"Who said anything about that? I just want you to know you're invited."

"Yeah, well, thanks but no thanks."

On Wednesday morning, Tyron told T.J. he was considering Notre Dame.

"Why is that?"

"Ishmael says I should think about it."

"Ishmael can go anywhere he wants," said T.J. while toweling his sweat and drinking cups of Gatorade. "Any college in the country would want him."

"Yeah, I know. He says I should think about it, though. That's why I'm considering Notre Dame."

"You can *consider* any place you want, but it's North State that made you the scholarship offer. They're the one that's considering *you*." Saying this, T.J. paused to speculate if there might be any connection between Notre Dame and Nike. He didn't know, though. He was beginning to wonder what was connected to what in order to form what networks.

"Ishmael thinks him 'n' me would make a great combination."

"You probably would. Hell, you already do; why do you think we've won six games the last two days?"

Tyron's grin seemed to reach from the left ear to the right ear. "You see me dunk on that gold team yesterday?"

"I saw. Listen, Bumpy—"

"No Bumpy!"

"Okay, sorry. Listen, Tyron, you have to think about loyalty too. Who was it that made you the first offer, huh? It was North State. Who was it that told us about Public Law 504 so you can have the ACT read to you?"

"I know, I know. It was Coach Lindsey at North State."

"Exactly. With all the bullshit that goes on, you have to think about loyalty."

"I still have the right to think about Notre Dame if I want to."

"Nobody says you don't." T.J. was fishing his watch from his athletic bag. He had at least forty minutes before the next game. "Do me a favor, though?"

"What favor?"

"Just keep away from Bee Edwards and those other street agents. Be sure you spend your time with Buddy and the guys. No hustlers."

"There's nothin' wrong with takin' shoes. Everybody gets shoes."

"Nobody gets shoes for nothin', Tyron."

"Nothin'. Not a cent, not even a nickel."

"It may not have anything to do with money. It might be a different kind of payoff;

just keep away from the street agents, okay?" Then T.J. left for the courts before he could hear what the answer might turn out to be.

The second game of the morning was another easy victory, but a disturbing clash developed between Tyron and Ishmael Greene. The other team was playing a box-and-one defense so as to free one man to shadow Greene wherever he might go. That wasn't a problem in itself, for no one person could cover Ishmael alone.

But the other players, none more so than Tyron, were enjoying their huge lead. They were basically standing around playing out the string, which left their defenders free to double- and even triple-team Ishmael. It was Ishmael alone who couldn't seem to find a way to put it on idle; it was a gear he didn't possess. He played with the same level of intense fury he might have needed in a tie game. With no warning at all, it seemed, he was all over Tyron for loafing. "How'm I s'posed to beat three guys?" he demanded to know.

"Huh?" said Tyron. He was grinning large and slapping high fives with his sated teammates.

"You need to house that motherfucker out the way; how'm I gonna drive the lane against my own man plus a three-man zone?" Ishmael was breathing hard, but he didn't appear tired. *It was almost like he couldn't get tired,* T.J. thought to himself. He also wondered why Ishmael chose to target Tyron, when the other players were on shutdown the same as he was.

"You don't need to get on Tyron's case," he said to Ishmael. "The game's over, for Christ sake."

"You see time left on that clock or not?" was Ishmael's response.

There was one minute and twelve seconds remaining on the small electric scoreboard next to the scorer's table. "I see a minute," T.J. replied. "I also see a thirty-point lead. Why don't you chill?"

"You see time on the clock, the game ain't over. You got that big ass of yours," he said to Tyron, "so house him out the lane. *I* need the lane, you understand?"

Tyron didn't understand. "Fuck you," he told Greene while gasping for breath. "I'm tired."

Buddy Ingalls interrupted when he declared, "That's enough. You all shut up. You don't coach, Ishmael, you just play. Any player needs to be told what to do, that's my job."

Ishmael flung down his towel without speaking and headed for the court. Before he sent him back into the game, Ingalls reminded Tyron, "Ishmael's right, though, Tyron. Coaches are everywhere you look; they don't want to think you've got quit in you."

"I'm so tired, though," said Tyron with the sweat running rivulets down his face and neck. "It's hot as hell."

"You heard what I said."

There were no more sparks after that, but T.J.'s relief was tempered by a measure of wariness. He was beginning to understand that it was more than talent alone that set Ishmael apart on the court. It was his unlimited intensity, his *passion* for competition that elevated him to the next level. But it was the same characteristic that could bring him into conflict with Tyron again.

FIVE

WHEN he went to the cafeteria, T.J. sought out a corner table that was a dumping ground for old newspapers. What he wanted was a place where he could be by himself and read sections of the *Peoria Journal-Star* and the *Chicago Tribune*, even if they were a day or two stale. He ate alone while reading an article about football players at Southeastern Conference schools who were suspended for betting on football games. After lunch, he made his way to the parking lot so he could spend some time in the Toyota. He flung the doors open for ventilation, sat in the passenger's seat, and opened the glove box. There were Marlboros in it, so he lit one up while he took out his diary. He turned to a fresh page, the one right after his record of the call Tyron had received from the De Paul coach. He decided to make a record of the information about Bee Edwards and the shoes, as well as his Notre Dame conversation with Tyron. As usual, he didn't know whether these entries would ever prove important or not; he simply wrote them down.

The voice he heard startled him: "Paperwork is never done, huh?"

When T.J. looked up he saw it was Coach Lindsey. He smiled. "I guess not, Coach."

Lindsey made a face. "Oh, Nucci, you're not smoking those things?"

"Not me, no sir."

"You don't want to, do you? Weren't you told it's against the rules?"

"I think I remember hearin' somethin' about it." Lindsey was wearing a white polo shirt with an Adidas logo. No wrinkles. No sweat. He was evenly tanned and handsome. T.J. said, "Okay, how about this? If you don't tell on me, I won't tell on you."

"Tell on me for what?"

"You're talkin' to me. Coaches aren't allowed

to do that. Even if it's only to me, a guy who doesn't have a college future as a player. I'm still one of the participants."

"Strictly speaking, that's right," confirmed the coach.

"Strictly speaking."

Coach Lindsey asked him, "Is that the diary?"

T.J. glanced down at the open book on his sweaty knees. "That's the diary," he acknowledged. "I was just reading the place where Tyron got a call from the De Paul coach."

"A call, you say?"

"That's what I said."

"You're not saying a letter, T.J.? You're saying Coach Kennedy called him on the phone?"

"He called him on the phone." The mysteries of the recruiting game were numerous, but T.J. didn't need to be told how important it was to receive a phone call from a major coach; a letter was just a matter of form, but the telephone was always the signal of serious interest.

Lindsey took a minute or two to absorb this information, as it was significant. Then he asked T.J. where Tyron stood relative to the ACT.

"That'll be up to Mrs. Osby," T.J. replied.

"Who's Mrs. Osby?" asked Lindsey, leaning against the car with his arms folded on his chest.

"She's a counselor at Burton. She's a kind of formal prude, but her heart's in the right place. At least I think it is."

"So what does she have to say about Tyron and the ACT?"

"You want to hear about this?" asked T.J.

"I asked, so I guess I do."

T.J. stubbed out the cigarette. He thought to himself, *as long as we're breaking the rules, why not do it large?* "Okay, here's what happened," he began.

His conversation with Mrs. Osby had occurred on a warm spring day on his very own front porch. He had simply been sitting there, reading a book for English class, when he chanced to see Mrs. Osby enter Tyron's huge, hodgepodge house on the corner. It was possible to see that far in spring before the trees were leafed out. He wondered why, exactly, Mrs. Osby would be there, but then she was a counselor at the high school where Tyron was a student. She probably had a place on the roster of all the advocates and specialists and social workers who managed the lives of young people living in group homes.

He had continued his reading long enough to give the porch post time to carve a sharp pain in his back. He would have gone inside, but he wanted to stay put until Mrs. Osby came out of the big house. When she finally did emerge, not until after 10:30, T.J. submitted to the urge to wave to her. Seeing him, she had crossed the street. She asked him if this was where he lived. He told her yes. She asked him if his mother was inside. He told her yes, but she was still in bed. "She works the night shift at Oblio's," he added.

"The pizzeria?"

"Yes. On weekend afternoons, she cleans office buildings."

"A hard worker. A very hard worker. Salt of the earth, it sounds like."

"I guess."

"May I join you for a few minutes?" Mrs. Osby had taken from her bag a cloth napkin with blue fringe, which was nearly as large as a dish towel. She shook it before she spread it carefully on the floorboards of the porch. When she seated herself squarely, she asked T.J. how long he'd known Tyron.

T.J. wondered about the big napkin, how she happened to have it ready like she knew she might need it. There were sharp creases in the legs of her navy blue pants suit. He thought of the woman lawyer in one of John Grisham's novels who wore camisoles all the time; it was an undergarment she wore to make sure her bra wouldn't show through her blouse. He figured Mrs. Osby would be no less circumspect in her manner of dress.

"Actually, I knew him back at Douglass High, in the city. I didn't know he was moving in that house until last summer."

"So the two of you were reunited, then?"

"In a way. I'm a lot closer to him now than I was back then."

"You want to advocate for him. You want to help him."

T.J. had realized quickly that her questions were going to require careful answers, and it wouldn't help matters much if they continued to come in the form of statements. The bottom line, he reminded himself, was that this was a woman you wanted on your side. He said, "It seems like somebody needs to give him a little help."

"Indeed. I'm afraid I don't know much about basketball. I take it Tyron is a good player?"

If you don't count the mental part, T.J. had thought to himself. "He's so good, he's had college coaches from all over watching him play. He's only a junior, but he averaged almost twenty-three points a game this season."

"He certainly is large. It would be basketball, then, which presumably would get him into college?"

"He'll get basketball scholarship offers," T.J. had replied.

"May I ask which schools are showing interest?"

"There's so many, it's hard to count. North State seems to be after him more than the rest."

"That's a major university. High entrance requirements and academic standards."

He had been careful not to argue with her, not even by mentioning the bonehead classes for athletes. "I guess."

"It seems a tricky business," Mrs. Osby observed, while taking a small notebook from her bag. "I've just been talking with him about school, his personal history, his goals, and so on. He's been through a lot, hasn't he?"

"Oh, yeah. He never knew his father, his mother was a druggie, I mean, what chance has he had in life?" *Back off*, T.J. warned himself. *It won't help to lay it on too thick.*

"It wouldn't seem like he's ready to tackle college work."

T.J. knew there was no way to counter this. But he could also tell that Mrs. Osby didn't understand about the kind of academic shelters given to college jocks. "He needs to work harder on his studies."

Mrs. Osby had opened a thin booklet that looked like it was made of newsprint. "Tyron and I went over some of the questions in the ACT practice book. We looked at them together, to try to establish the kind of material included in the test."

T.J. didn't say a word. He was afraid to.

Mrs. Osby continued, "I wish I could say that he showed a solid grasp, at least in general."

"The ACT is tough," said T.J. "Especially under a time limit."

Now she was looking him in the eye, but T.J. returned her gaze. "T.J., your friend thinks the faces carved in Mount Rushmore are accidents of nature. He thinks those faces are miracles of wind and rain."

"You mean that's not true?"

Mrs. Osby laughed with a kind of gay, ringing sound. It was the first time she had seemed attractive. T.J. could imagine she might have been a babe in her day.

"I see you have humor," she had continued. "Tyron also thinks that Washington, D.C., and Washington State are the same place."

"Did he say centigrade or Fahrenheit?" Not that it was actually funny, not that he wanted to be flippant, but the bottom line of this conversation had become apparent. Mrs. Osby had a reputation as a kind soul, but even she could see how far out it would be to picture Bumpy enrolled in a university.

But then she said, "It's clear that something is wrong."

"Something is wrong? I'm not sure I understand."

"Of course something is wrong," Mrs. Osby enlarged. "A student doesn't come this ill-prepared to the end of his junior year for no reason. It should be clear to any of us that the system has failed him along the way. Or should I say systems, plural?"

"I'm not sure I follow you." *Could the negative be the positive?*

"Instead of assuming that the fault lies in the student, we need always to ask ourselves if the system itself has met his needs. In other words, a student who has such a view of Mount Rushmore has probably not been given adequate educational opportunities."

"I see."

"That's what I meant when I said something must be wrong."

"I see," T.J. repeated himself. At this point, a link had formed in his mind between this conversation and the first heart-to-heart he'd had with Coach Lindsey from North State. He asked Mrs. Osby, "You're saying he hasn't had enough opportunities."

"I don't know where his opportunities would have occurred. Certainly not in the home. As for Douglass High, I don't have to tell you that Chicago schools are plagued with the kind of social problems that inhibit quality education. All manner of standardized testing results confirm that."

T.J. was listening hard and sitting up straight, and not only because of the pain in his back. If this didn't sound like 504, he didn't know what would.

Mrs. Osby was putting the printed matter back in her bag. "He may never have been properly tested along the way, or he may not have been tested at all," she said. "The system is designed to include a safety net, but a net has lots of holes."

Dare I say it? T.J. had asked himself. Then he did, anyway. "He may have slipped through the cracks."

"If you like cracks better than holes," she said with another laugh. "In any case, that's the point."

T.J. had decided to push the envelope by one more increment: "Did you know that college athletes have daily tutoring and help with their academics? It's called a support system."

"That's another important element in the mix, then. Support systems are crucial for at-risk students."

"Does this mean you'll read the ACT to him?"

"I can't make a promise at this point, but it certainly bears looking into."

When he was finished with the story, T.J. looked up at Coach Lindsey, who was still propped against the side of the car, wearing the same slouching posture.

"That's where it stands?" asked the coach.

"Right now, that's where it stands. What d'you think?"

"I think you made a short story long. That's more details than I need."

"Sorry. You had to be there, though."

Lindsey seemed pensive, the way he was squeezing on his chin. "If she reads him the test, when will that be?"

"The end of September, I think. Maybe it's October; I can't remember for sure."

"Something to think about, isn't it?" mused the coach. He was still squeezing his chin, but not looking in T.J.'s direction. Instead, he was staring at the right rear tire.

Lindsey's response was disappointing to T.J., who was hoping that this possibility in connection with the ACT would trigger some enthusiasm. He decided to keep his mouth shut, though.

The coach was looking at his watch. "You've got another game, don't you?"

"Not for five minutes yet. I'll be okay." In a way, it bothered him too that Lindsey wasn't asking about other parts of his diary. While he put the book away in the glove box, he found himself thinking ever so briefly of the girl on the bridge. What was her name? LuAnn, wasn't it?

"Don't be late for tip-off, Nucci."

"Yeah, yeah, I'll be there, don't worry."

He might not have seen her again at all, except he chose to. That is to say, he chose to try. First, though, they had to get through the game against a team called the Blazers, made up primarily of players from the Quad Cities and Quincy.

Since it was their second game of the evening, it didn't start until dusk. At least it was cooler when you played under the lights, thought T.J., but the game brought out the worst in Tyron. He was matched against a wiry jumping jack named Sweeney, who was relentless. He wasn't a good shooter, but he was extremely active and focused. During the first half alone, Sweeney blocked at least three of Tyron's jump shots and outhustled him for inside rebounds.

T.J.'s own assignment wasn't tough at all. Playing one of the wings in a one-three-one zone, all he had to do was check a slow white guy who wanted to shoot threes but wasn't inclined to do much of anything else. He wasn't athletic enough to break you down, so all you had to do was overguard him on the perimeter.

In the second half, Tyron was not a factor; he was discouraged and intimidated. He was sluggish, slow down the court, and drained of intensity.

"Big post, Tyron!" Buddy Ingalls kept hollering at him. "Big post! Take it up strong!"

Once, when Ishmael Greene was huffing and puffing past the bench, he said to Ingalls, "Take him out the game." He was referring to Tyron, of course.

There was no big post, no effective dropstepping, and no going up strong. The way Tyron folded his tent when he was challenged was a thing no college scout could ignore. In short, he was the player he used to be, the player T.J. hoped would not show up at this camp.

When he was sitting on the bench, T.J. couldn't help noticing how Coach Lindsey had turned his back to watch the action on the other courts. He cautioned himself not to make too big a deal out of that, though, because there were more than 160 players here, and at least 50 of them were major talents.

With five minutes remaining, Tyron was slumped on the bench and burying his head in the most available towel. Even the new shoes didn't help. Ishmael Greene was magnificent, but he wasn't enough; the Blazer lead continued to grow until the end of the game. For the first time, the Blue Stars lost.

When he took his shower back at the dorm, T.J. allowed enough time to shave the few chin whiskers he had, brush his teeth, and put on some Old Spice aftershave. He even combed his hair. He put on a pair of shorts and a clean New Jersey Nets jersey with GILL 13 lettering on the back. Tyron asked him if he was going down to watch the movie.

"No thanks."

"Where you goin', man?"

"Out," said T.J.

"They're showin' *Forrest Gump*."

"That's okay, I don't want to watch it. You go see it."

SIX

WHEN T.J. got to the bridge, it was after dark. Since it took almost sixty paces to reach the middle, he figured the bridge itself must be at least two hundred feet long. His vision was limited because the only strong light came from the pole lights.

While he leaned against the rough railing, he could hear the singing and shouting from the religious meeting on the other side. He thought of LuAnn and his curiosity got the better of him; he crossed over the rest of the way.

There were crude concrete steps set in the slope leading down to a walking path. There was less available light the farther you descended, so you had to watch your step. T.J.

had to wonder again what it was that drew him in the direction of the lighted pavilion at the far end of the path. The Religious Right usually pissed him off; especially the self-righteous geeks who held hands and prayed around the flagpole in the parking lot before school in the morning. Then went around whining most of the day because they weren't allowed to read scripture in class, like you couldn't study history or physics unless you had a Bible reading to get you kick-started.

It was something about LuAnn, he guessed, some hard-to-define need to know her better; either that or just the need to put some distance between himself and the Blue Stars for a while.

The pavilion, he discovered as he drew nearer, was larger than he'd expected. It had a peaked roof supported by rough-hewn, wooden columns, but no walls. T.J. estimated the crowd at more than two hundred people, most of them as young as himself, seated on wooden benches arranged in rows on both sides of a center aisle. The adults in the audience would have to be counselors or sponsors. Many of them were clapping their hands or holding their arms in the air like a football referee signaling a touch-down.

There were enough ceiling lights in the pavilion that T.J. had to keep a distance so he could conceal himself in the darkness made by the dense trees near the walking path. The speaker on the stage was a beautiful woman in a white gown who was wearing a clip-on microphone. She delivered much of her speech with her eyes closed and her arms raised.

"Death will have no dominion," she was telling the listeners, "when the Rapture comes. On that blessed day we will join the Lord in the air. Those who know the Lord, those who belong to His flock, He will take unto Himself. Those who mingle with the goats will be left behind; know now who are the sheep and who are the goats, for the company you keep today will determine how you will spend eternity."

The woman was beautiful, especially in the glow of the track lighting suspended from the ceiling above her position on the stage. She didn't speak aggressively, in a fire-and-brimstone mode, but with a certain mystical serenity. She repeated her assurance that "In the Lord's flock, Death will have no dominion. That is his promise to us."

The long, reddish-blond hair that rested on her shoulders shimmered in the light; the lettering on the front of her gown constituted an optical trick—what looked like a haphazard maze of Magic Marker lines when her body was turned in one direction formed the word JESUS in capital letters when she turned another.

Her mesmerizing presence caused T.J. to stay longer than he intended. By the time he thought to slip away, the woman was finished speaking and people were leaving the shelter. There were massive tree roots where he stood, which threatened to trip him up, so he moved slowly near the others, in the direction of the bridge, hoping nobody would speak to him and LuAnn wouldn't notice him.

It didn't work. She spotted him and in a loud voice called, "T.J.! Over here, T.J."

He felt like an idiot. He wanted only to get away as quickly as possible, but he couldn't pretend like he hadn't heard her voice. He came to a stop while she approached. "You came," she declared.

"Just don't try to convert me," he said tightly, in a low voice.

"You came," she repeated. "Why did you come?"

"I have no idea." He turned to face her. Her large breasts nicely filled out a T-shirt with a graphic portrayal of the crucifixion; the lettering below the artwork proclaimed, THIS BLOOD'S FOR YOU.

"I really didn't expect you to come," she said, beaming. "Why did you come?"

"I already told you, I have no idea. I guess it was just curiosity. It's an old habit of mine. I better be going now."

"Please, I want you to meet Sister Simone first."

T.J. didn't know which one Sister Simone was, but he guessed it was the speaker. "No, I better go," he said again. "If they find out I went AWOL, they might bench me."

It was irony lost on LuAnn. She gripped his hand. "Come on," she tugged. "Just for a minute. I want you to meet her."

There were other people around; it was easier to submit than to break away from her and make a scene. He let himself be pulled to the edge of the pavilion where Sister Simone was tucking some folded papers inside a well-worn Bible.

LuAnn conducted the introduction while they shook hands. Sister Simone was an inch or so taller than T.J. and even more beautiful up close than from a distance. Her complexion was clear and her makeup was expertly applied. She looked straight into his eyes as she said, "I'm happy to meet you, T.J."

"The same here," he mumbled awkwardly, and then he asked her why her name was Sister. "Are you, like, a nun or something?"

Sister Simone laughed before she replied. "Something like that, you could say. At Camp Shaddai, we're all simply brothers and sisters in Christ."

"Oh, yeah."

"Ruth Ann was talking about you earlier today," Sister Simone informed him.

"Who is Ruth Ann?" he asked.

"That's me," said LuAnn, with a giggle and a smile.

"How is it you?" T.J. asked her. "You told me your name was LuAnn."

"It's my new name in Christ. We submit to the will of the Lord in all things. The new name we choose is a symbol of that submission."

"Yeah, okay." T.J. was sure he couldn't stand any more. The annoying smiles were everywhere like a rock in your shoe. Already, he didn't trust the glamorous woman who called herself Sister Simone, which was nuts; he'd only just met her. "I better go now."

Sister Simone added to LuAnn (Ruth Ann's) explanation: "Choosing the new name is like putting off our old self so we can put on the new self of God."

T.J. felt himself tighten up in exasperation. "I better get the hell out of here," he said quickly. "No offense, Sister."

Simone laughed gaily, with the perfect white teeth of a movie star. "None taken," she said. "Getting the hell out is what we do best. Camp Shaddai is a very uncomfortable place for Satan, I'm afraid."

He left without another word, walking briskly on the path that would take him back to the bridge. He felt foolish and regretted ever coming to this side at all.

By the time he reached the center of the bridge, he had succeeded, through a conscious effort of the will, in focusing his thoughts on Tyron, Coach Lindsey, Bee Edwards, and the rest of the Full Court soap opera. The street agents, the rules, and how he would ever find a way to guard Ronnie Streets.

T.J. lit one of his cigarettes and took a seat close to the edge. In the dark, he listened for the sounds of moving water in the creek bed far below, but there were none. Within a few minutes, though, he heard LuAnn's footsteps squeaking the floorboards. It didn't surprise him that she had followed him, but why was it he expected that she would? *How could you know a person without really knowing them?* he wondered.

"You must be all basketballed out," she observed. "Maybe that's why you came."

"I guess so." She was taking a seat beside him. He tossed his lit cigarette butt casually so as to watch it tumble clear down to the bottom of the gorge like a firecracker.

"Don't you think Sister Simone is real spiritual?"

"I guess you could call it that." It was easier than saying what he really thought.

"She's blessed with all kinds of spiritual gifts; mostly she has the gift of prophecy."

"Do you really believe all that stuff?" T.J. asked her.

Her smile disappeared, but her eyes were still wide. "All what stuff?"

"That stuff about the Rapture. About joining the Lord in the air."

"Of course."

"Never dying."

"Of course. We have God's word on it."

"But I mean do you, like, *really* believe it?"

There must have been some exasperation in his voice, because she giggled before she replied, "I guess the Lord must want you to be crabby."

"Sorry," said T.J.

"It's in the Book of Revelation, so it's part of God's promise. A promise from God is easy to believe. The hard thing would be what you do, which is believe in something else."

"How do you know what I believe?"

They fell silent for a few moments, during which time T.J. was annoyed by a sense of his own incompetence. He couldn't think of any real value in conversations like this one, which were basically just for taking up space.

Politely, she asked him about his family.

"There's just my mother and me."

"Does she have a job?"

"She has two jobs."

"She must be a very hard worker."

"She *is* a very hard worker. On her days off, she goes fishing sometimes. She never complains and she's never been on welfare."

"You admire her, don't you?"

"I guess I do. She's also enrolled in a computer course in night school. She's trying to learn a financial program so she can apply for this corporate job she's got her eye on."

LuAnn (Ruth Ann) asked him why they moved to Burton from Chicago.

"We had to get out of the city. We had to get away from my stepfather because he used to beat her up. She was under a protection order, but it didn't work. They never do."

"Ouch. I asked, didn't I?"

"Sometimes he used to beat me up too. Once I coldcocked him, though. I'll never forget it. I was about twelve, maybe eleven. Anyway, he had ahold of her by the arms when I came up from behind and tapped him on the shoulder. He turned around to see who it was and I got him. One time, right in the mouth, with all my force. He had blood comin' out of his mouth, and loose teeth and all, but the best thing of it was that look on his face. It was, like, total *shock*, you know what I mean?"

"Then what happened?"

His own blunt, aggressive mode was puzzling to him. He didn't know if it was because he was trying to navigate a conversation without a compass, or if it really did piss him off to think about Lloyd again. "He beat the shit out of me," T.J. finally admitted, in a more subdued tone of voice. "But I still got him. At least that one time, I coldcocked the son of a bitch."

"Does your mother need someone to pray for her?" She took his hand while asking the question.

"Does she need what?"

"Because we have a prayer chain. We could put her on it."

T.J. disengaged his hand and looked away.

Have I ever been in a stupider conversation?
He knew he ought to leave. Instead, he said,
"Listen, LuAnn, you need to get real. There
are people who take care of themselves. It's
called depending on your own resources."

"Our own resources aren't good enough. I
came to Camp Shaddai because I need to put
my trust in the Lord completely."

"That's another thing. How did you get
here, anyway, and are you, like, here for good?"

"Nobody stays at Camp Shaddai forever.
I'll just be here until I find my way."

"So how did you get here, then?"

"Brother Jackson brought me."

"Who's that?" T.J. asked her.

"He's an evangelist. He's real, real spiritual.
He has a tabernacle in Peoria, but he also trav-
els around on preaching missions. Right now
he's in Missouri or Oklahoma or someplace."

"So why did he bring you here? What's he
to you?"

LuAnn (Ruth Ann) had her arms folded
over the railing again. Her chin rested firmly on
her right wrist. "Because I asked him to. I
needed a place to get away; I needed a retreat."

"A retreat for what?"

"A retreat so I could sort things out. With no distractions."

"Sort what things?"

Then she told him, "I was pregnant."

"*Was* pregnant?"

"*Am* pregnant. I'm pregnant right now."

She didn't look it, though, T.J. thought. But why would she lie about it? "You know what?" he said. "My advice to you would be, keep private things private."

Her face was expressionless, but there were tears rolling down her face. "And why is that?"

"It gives people power if they know too much about you. They can use the power to take advantage of you. Who's the father?"

"You just told me to keep private things private."

"Yeah, that's true. Sorry I asked."

"It doesn't matter who the father is," she continued. "It's my sin, no matter who the man is."

Her casual use of the word *sin* seemed ominous to T.J. This conversation had gone from irrelevant to a trip on the dark side. It was time to give it up. A glance at his watch told him it was 10:20, well past their curfew. "I'd better go," he said.

"My advice to you," said LuAnn, "would be to learn a little bit about trust."

"Maybe, but I'm telling you the truth. That's the way people are."

"Sometimes they are," she agreed. "That's why I need to be here at Camp Shaddai, where our trust is in the Lord, not in men."

"You want someone to tell you what to do?" He stood up and started brushing off the seat of his pants. The things that needed his attention were trying to guard Ronnie Streets the next time he had to, and resuscitating Tyron's motivation.

"I don't want *someone* to tell me what to do," LuAnn replied, without looking in his direction. "I want to know the Lord's will. I want *Him* to tell me what to do."

SEVEN

RIGHT from the start, Friday was a bad day. After breakfast, when he went into the coaches' dining room to scrounge for the newspaper, all T.J. could find was the women's section and the comics. He waved at Coach Lindsey, but the coach avoided eye contact. To make anything out of that, though, would just be paranoid.

Tyron had a brand-new pair of sweats, with the Reebok logo. He showed the sweats to T.J. as they made their way to the courts. "Bee Edwards again?" asked T.J.

"No, it wasn't Bee this time. A guy named McLemore gave them to me."

"And who's McLemore? Not that I really want to know."

"I don't know who he is, he's just a guy."

"Nobody's just a *guy*, Tyron. Even people who *don't* give you things aren't just a guy."

Ishmael Greene said, "He's just another hustler. Like Bee Edwards and all the rest of 'em. It's nothin'."

"He gives sweats away," muttered T.J.

"Sweats, shoes, whatever. Ain't no rule against it. Why don't you just chill?"

T.J. said, "You see what bullshit this is? There's supposed to be a *Converse* school or a *Nike* school, like a college is a store or an outlet for a shoe company. You can't see how that's bullshit?"

Ishmael shrugged. "Ain't no rule against it," he simply repeated.

With an air of vindication, Tyron tucked his new sweats carefully under his arm as he announced he was considering the University of Illinois.

"Is that so?" asked T.J. "Why is that?"

"Obie was tellin' me about the Hall."

"What about the Hall?"

"It's like Madison Square Garden. It's like the United Center. Tell him, Obie, tell T.J."

Obie Williams explained, "We were just

talkin' about the Hall. Once you see the Assembly Hall, you know it's the primo place to play."

"Shit," said Ishmael.

"I've been there," said T.J. "I've seen it. It's a great arena, but so what? There's lots of great arenas."

"But not like the Hall."

"Are you goin' there?" T.J. asked Obie.

"If they offer, but they haven't offered yet," Obie answered.

Tyron repeated his new goal: "Anyway, I think I'm considerin' the U of I."

T.J. was exasperated. "You have no idea what you're sayin', Big Guy. Have you ever heard of the Summer Bridge program?"

"No. What's that?"

"It's summer school, Tyron, before they'll even let you in. Before you even get to start your freshman year."

"I went to summer school this year, though."

"It's not the same thing; you took one course for six weeks. I'm talkin' English, math, and science, from sunup to sundown. In the summer."

"You're bullshittin' me now," said Tyron, "You're just makin' it up."

"I'm *not* makin' it up. Ask Ishmael."

"It's true, Tyron," Ishmael confirmed. "He's tellin' you the truth."

"But what if I pass my ACT? If Mrs. Osby helps me, I might pass it."

"Don't matter," Ishmael told him. "Even if you pass the test, they'll still make you go through the Bridge."

"But that sucks."

"Tell me. It's like jail, man. School all day and night, you don't even get time off for workin' out. T.J. is not lyin' to you."

"But that sucks if you pass your ACT." Tyron wore his disappointment plainly on his face. He looked in Obie's direction for some reassurance. "You never said nothin' about this."

Obie shook his head before saying, "We were talkin' about the Hall, man. Don't worry, there's plenty of schools with no bridge program."

"For sure," said Ishmael with a laugh. He slapped Tyron on the back. "There's plenty for sure."

It was a relief to T.J. when he saw that Tyron's U of I agenda would ebb even quicker than it flowed. He was nearly at the point of indifference regarding the sweats and shoes and street agents.

The problem now was winning and losing.

By this point in the week, the preoccupation with winning as a team was escalating. Earlier, simply playing well as an individual and impressing scouts seemed enough to satisfy any participant. But no longer. By winning so many games, the Blue Stars were in the championship fight, and the predatory competitiveness that prevailed in players at this level was off the leash. Winning was everything.

As far as T.J. was concerned, it was an unhappy development. He didn't have the skills—or the inclination—to compete with these people, but with such an emphasis on winning, he would be expected to be a more productive player.

After winning their first game of the morning, they were now in a unique position. Since they had only one loss, they could win the championship by beating their next opponent, a talented team comprised mostly of players from the Gary, Indiana, area. If they lost, they would still be in a position to win the championship the next day.

Not too many minutes into the game, one of the guards, Evans, suffered an asthma attack. It wasn't his first, but it was the worst. He was taken to the first aid building to recover. His absence meant more playing time for T.J.—much more.

The game was close for a while, until Tyron lost his intensity and T.J. was sucking wind. He was trying to guard a gazelle named Curtis Lore, who broke him down in every direction. T.J. was getting the shakes trying to chase him, and his ankle began to hurt again. It wasn't a disabling injury, not even an injury at all in the purest sense of the term, and certainly not the kind of thing to keep you out of the lineup. But the nagging pain was a distraction.

Once, during a time-out, he begged Buddy Ingalls to let them play a zone.

"No way," said Ingalls. "We're not playin' that pussy shit."

"But it's good strategy," argued T.J.

"It's good strategy for pussies. No pain, no gain, *amigo*."

T.J. groaned inwardly. Hadn't he used the same line on Tyron often enough?

In the second half, Ishmael Greene pushed his intensity up a notch or two higher, which you wouldn't have thought possible, but everybody could see it. He played like a man possessed. By trying to compensate for his team's own disadvantaged condition, though, he got himself into foul trouble.

T.J. was grabbing his shorts and fighting for breath at every opportunity. At least this was a game where they were shooting free throws, so there were occasional stops in the action. He kept looking in the direction of the first aid building, hoping to see Evans headed back in their direction and fully recovered from the asthma attack. But no such luck.

Finally, with about six minutes remaining, T.J. tried desperately to stay with Curtis Lore in a fast-break situation. It was hopeless. Lore went over him and dunked in his face. T.J. went to his knees. The sweat was pouring from his face; his heart was pounding so hard in his chest, he felt like he was on the verge of cardiac arrest. The blood was slamming in his temples.

When Buddy Ingalls asked him if it was the ankle again, T.J. answered breathlessly. "Yeah," he lied. "It's the ankle."

"D'you have to come out?"

"Yeah. I have to come out."

He sat on the bench with a cold, wet towel draped over his head. Buddy asked him if he needed to go to the first aid building, but T.J. said he could wait until the game was over. He didn't move the towel when he answered the question. His early departure meant Obie had to go back in, but with four fouls.

Obie fouled out quickly, but it took Ishmael a little longer. He didn't get the fifth one until three and a half minutes were left. They were behind by five points. Then the other team stretched the lead to twelve so fast, it made your head spin. Ishmael was breathing hard in the seat next to T.J., but T.J. didn't want to talk to him; he kept his towel in place.

Ishmael's voice was low, but T.J. could hear him: "You quit on us, Nucci."

T.J. lifted his head and pulled the towel back to drape it around his neck. His breathing was nearly normal. "You talkin' to me?"

"You see anybody else got your name? We could've won the game, but you quit on us."

T.J. looked at the rivers of sweat crisscrossing Ishmael's ebony face before he answered. "Who gives a rat's ass about winning this game?"

"There ain't nothin' *to* do but win, know what I mean?"

"This is a summer game. It doesn't mean a thing."

"Ain't no such thing as a game not to win."

"Who gives a shit, Ishmael? You're a super-star, you can get a scholarship anywhere you want. Notre Dame or wherever."

Ishmael was toweling the sweat from his face and neck. He said, "You know what you are, T.J.? You're a spook. A spook is somebody who don't come to play."

"Fuck you, Ishmael."

"Either a spook or another one of these hangin' around street agents. I can't figure out which."

It was too much. "Fuck *you*, Ishmael!" Then

T.J. hit him. He doubled his fist and punched him hard on his right ear. It was the wrong thing to do for any number of reasons, not the least of which was Ishmael's greater size and strength. Ishmael took him down on the tartan surface, which felt as hard as old-fashioned blacktop, and would have punched him in the face. Except there were so many people pulling the two of them apart.

"Fuck you, spook!" Ishmael screamed while being restrained by three guys, including Buddy Ingalls.

When the commotion subsided, Ingalls took T.J. to the first aid building. Not a word passed between them. T.J. sat with his head down while Bridget put on a pair of latex gloves to examine the back of his head. Evans was sound asleep on the other table. T.J. was sweating again, and getting the shakes, symptoms of the aftermath from the violent encounter with Ishmael.

In addition to these shocklike symptoms, his head hurt and so did his ankle, even if only on a subacute level. None of it was significant, however, not compared to his inner turmoil of guilt and shame. *He called me a street agent.*

Bridget, the girl who did the crosswords, was picking at the back of his scalp, searching through his hair for the two minor cuts she would find, along with the morsel of tartan court about the size of a BB. "Does this hurt?" she asked him.

"Does what hurt?"

"I'm probing around on these cuts. Does it hurt?"

T.J. nearly laughed, it seemed so absurd. The thing that hurt was the thing she could never see: Ishmael's accusations.

He didn't plan to see LuAnn again; he only went to the bridge to be alone in the dark. He certainly wasn't thinking about her, or anyone else not connected with the basketball camp.

When he did see her, though, he couldn't have known it would be for the last time. The squeaking floorboards startled him; he hadn't seen her coming. "I kinda thought you'd be here," she told him as she sat down beside him.

"I didn't," he answered. "I just needed to be by myself."

"You want me to leave?"

"No; stay."

"You haven't told anyone, have you?"

"About you? I haven't said a word to anyone."

She asked him, "What does the T.J. stand for?"

"T is for Thomas, J is for John."

LuAnn's head rested on her forearms, which were positioned on the lower railing. "Those are biblical names," she observed.

"You mean I got the right answer?"

"You don't have to be sarcastic." She was giggling, though. "It's just that biblical names are special; that's why I like Ruth Ann so much better than LuAnn."

It didn't work for T.J., however. He lit a cigarette before he said, "You can't just run away, though."

"Do you think I'm running away?"

"I don't want to hurt your feelings or anything, but I don't know what else you'd call it. If you've got problems, even if it's a major one like being knocked up, you have to find a way to face up to it."

"I'm not running away," she protested,

"I'm running *to*. I'm running to the Lord for guidance."

"And that's another thing. Just because you run away with a preacher, that doesn't make it any different. Know what I mean?"

"I didn't run away with Brother Jackson. He just brought me here. He's in Oklahoma or Missouri now."

"Is he the father?"

The question was too blunt or too irrelevant, apparently. She turned her face away. "It doesn't matter."

"Okay, I'm sorry for asking."

"You don't have to apologize. It's just that it doesn't matter because it's my own sin, no matter who the father is."

"I don't see why it has to have anything to do with sin," said T.J.

When she turned to face him again, her smile was back in place. "Do you believe in dreams?" she asked.

"What's not to believe? People have dreams."

"No, but do you believe dreams have meanings?"

"They're supposed to have a subconscious meaning, at least according to psychiatrists."

"It's not psychiatry that I care about, though. It's the Lord's will. If you believe that the Lord speaks to you in dreams, He can direct your thoughts and actions."

"Really," said T.J.

LuAnn went on, "I've had a dream twice this week about the pale horse. Over and over, I saw this white horse running across the footbridge."

"This footbridge?"

"This very one. He was so loud! His hooves were just pounding and pounding on the boards. It was very hollow sounding and very loud. His body was all sweaty and the sweat was foaming him over like lather."

Her sense of urgency at this point increased T.J.'s interest, in spite of himself. "It sounds like something from the Bible," he said.

"There's a passage from Revelation, chapter six. It says, 'And I looked, and behold a pale horse: and his name that sat on him was Death, and Hell followed after him.'"

"Okay, then that explains it—you had a dream about the Bible."

"You don't understand Spirit-filled living, though, T.J. The Gifts of the Spirit can enlighten us beyond our mortal understanding."

"You're right, I don't understand Spirit-filled living. I don't even know what it is."

Her smile was still there, while the dream-like countenance might have been merely a haloed effect from the feeble available light. She wanted him to understand. "I've had the dream twice, which tells me the Lord wants to work through me. It's really very blessed. Now I need help to interpret the dream, but Sister Simone is here to help me. She has the Gift of interpretation, as well as the Gift of prophecy."

"What about the gift of IQ? I mean your own brain."

"I asked you not to be sarcastic."

"It seems pretty simple to me," T.J. declared. "You spend all day studying the Bible, so why wouldn't you dream about it at night?"

"Yes, but if only you could someday be baptized in the Spirit, you might understand. That's what I think of when I pray for you."

"You pray for me?" T.J. was flabbergasted. His own confusion made it impossible to know where his impatience was rooted. Nevertheless, he said, "I gotta tell you, LuAnn, this all sounds like a lot of political bullshit to me."

"What are you talking about?"

"I'm talkin' about the whole thing. The preacher who brings you here, the counselor who says she's never going to die. I mean, why doesn't somebody like just tell you to go home and work things out with your parents?"

"You don't even know Sister Simone. How can you talk about her?" Her smile was gone.

T.J. couldn't deny what she said. He *didn't* know Sister Simone, so if she gave him bad vibes, even if the whole Bible camp itself did, what did it prove? He really didn't know anything about it. He finally said, "I'm sorry if I hurt your feelings. It just doesn't seem right to me." *If I fucked up with Ishmael and with Tyron, I might as well fuck up here too.*

"T.J., I'm talking about surrendering to the Lord Himself, so why would you bring up politics?"

The answer seemed easy. "Everything in life seems like politics to me right now."

"It's crazy, though, isn't it? Me talking about

gifts from the Holy Spirit, and you bringing up Republicans and Democrats."

"You think politics is about *Congress*? Is that what you think? That's not even the tip of the iceberg. Politics is when you can manipulate systems to your own benefit. It's how you get power."

"You mean like kissing up."

"I mean exactly like kissing up. If it gets you power you can use, it's political."

LuAnn had her headband off; she was redefining the folds so that all the letters would be fully visible. When the headband was back in place, she put her hand on his arm. "I'm still going to pray for you."

T.J. said, "Thank you." He couldn't think of anything else.

"You hurt my feelings, but that only means I haven't surrendered completely. I know you mean well. Your heart is in the right place. I'm sure the Lord will bless you for it."

She was smiling again.

EIGHT

THE first game was easy, but everyone knew it would be. T.J. blended in without exerting himself. When Evans's asthma began acting up again, he needed to play more but it didn't matter—he was pacing himself. Ishmael Greene was his usual splendid self, but since the game was so lopsided, he spent most of the last quarter on the bench. Buddy wanted to rest him for the championship game, which came later.

Tyron had a monster game, even if the opposition was inferior. He had four dunks and a host of rebounds. When he was seated on the bench, and during time-outs, T.J. kept to himself; he took no part in the high-fiving or the yukking it up.

During the one-hour break before the championship game, T.J. went to the first aid building to get his ankle taped. The camp doctor was there, examining Evans. T.J. sat on the table while Bridget taped his ankle tight with one careful layer after another.

From this position, he could see—just barely—to the far bluff and the west end of the footbridge. There was a commotion that looked like sheriff's cars and an ambulance, but it was hard to tell for sure. It looked as if sheriffs' deputies were putting a barricade at the entrance to the bridge.

It was all too far away to determine exactly what might be occurring, but what he could make out gave him a queasy feeling. It could be anything, though. Most likely, the queasy feeling was only the by-product he often felt when there was information he thought he needed but couldn't get.

When she was done taping him, Bridget said, "By the way, I looked up the word *feckless*. There is such a word."

"So what's it mean?"

"You wanta know, you can look it up like I did."

"Thanks a lot."

Before he left the building, T.J. heard the doctor tell Evans, "I think you need to sit this one out, son. I'm sorry."

The Blue Stars won the championship game by more than ten points. One reason why—a big one—was the way T.J. played. He wasn't the star of the game by any stretch; he scored only nine points. But he understood what he needed to provide to give his own team an advantage—defense.

Guarding Ronnie Streets was like chasing butterflies without a net, but T.J. found himself at a level of focused intensity as consuming as it was unfamiliar. He refused to let Streets break him down. He refused to let fatigue undermine his concentration, which was footwork. If he could force Streets to shoot perimeter jump shots, where he was only average, then he could check him.

It worked even better than he dared to hope. As soon as Streets missed some jump shots, he began trying to do too much. He shot too much. He forced plays that weren't there, throwing the ball away. His too-aggressive defense got him in foul trouble. Wherever he went on the court, with or without the ball, there was T.J., dogging him as tenaciously as a shadow.

Even though he got only two brief rests on the bench, T.J. refused to give in to pain or fatigue. There was no shortness of breath and no sore ankle, there was only the path to Streets, whether direct or around a series of screens.

It was late in the game when Streets attempted a highlight-film dunk on the fast break, but there was T.J. locked in perfect position to take the charge. The basket didn't count; Streets had fouled out of the game.

After that, the lead swelled quickly. T.J. got to sit out the last three minutes with the starters. Right next to Ishmael, who told him, "Nice game, man."

T.J. was too short of breath for more than a one-word answer: "Thanks."

"What I said yesterday was wrong, man. I'm sorry. You can play."

T.J. didn't answer. He lowered his head and draped the wet towel to hide his face. He had tears forming in his eyes that he didn't want anyone to see. In the contemplative days and weeks ahead, he would ponder (among other things) how it was that he came to play such a great game. A game so much better than he had ever played before or imagined he could play. What blend of guilt, frustration, shame, and desperation caught upon this point in time? Might he have had this talent all along but no sufficient motivation to focus it? And what, if anything, about the girl on the bridge? There would be so many questions but so few answers.

Just as the game was winding down, but before the high fives began, T.J. said to Ishmael, "You don't have to apologize, Ishmael. You were right."

"I was wrong, man. You can play."

Ishmael saw what he needed to see. T.J. dropped the subject. He turned to look in the direction of the footbridge. It wasn't easy to see from here, but the space between the branches showed him there was yellow tape fixed to the railings on the far side, the kind used by police to seal off the scene of a crime or accident. He felt queasy in the stomach again.

Back in the dorm, they packed their gear. Some of the guys were in a hurry because they were being picked up by parents or other relatives. T.J. was in a hurry because he wanted to be out of here; he wanted to put distance between himself and Full Court as soon as he could. He felt like if he never played basketball again, he wouldn't have any regrets.

"Can't you hurry, Big Guy?" he urged Tyron.

Tyron was using a pair of the new shoes to establish a partition so he could separate the clean clothes from the dirty ones in his huge duffel bag. "I'm hurryin' already," he replied.

"Why don't you see if you can hurry faster?"

The heavy vegetation surrounding the road out formed a tunnel that led back to reality, as far as he was concerned, and he was eager to follow it there. He was driving too fast, though, and it wasn't long before he noticed he was low on gas and the engine was overheating.

He pulled sharply into the gravel parking lot of Heaven's Gate.

"Not this place again," Tyron said, and

groaned. He seemed exhausted. He squirmed in his seat, striving in vain for additional room.

"It's only for a few minutes. We need gas, and the radiator's overheatin'."

Tyron gave T.J. three crumpled-up one-dollar bills. "Get me a bag of nachos, okay, T.J.?"

"Okay."

"And I'll take a Moon Pie too, if they have 'em. One Moon Pie and a bag of nachos."

"Okay, okay."

Inside, the light was low and the Garth Brooks hit was loud on the jukebox. Two guys were shooting pool. Beyond the pinball machine, some of the coaches from Full Court were hoisting beers and engaged in loud conversation.

The redneck guy behind the cash register was wearing overalls without a shirt and a hunting cap. He had a burn scar next to his left eyebrow. When T.J. told him he needed gas and water, the guy brought out a battered metal can with a spout from behind the counter. "Faucet's on the north side of the building," he declared.

"I need some gas too," said T.J.

"Turning it on now," was the answer.

As soon as he was finished pumping the gas and adding water to the radiator, T.J. went inside to pay. Coach Lindsey, holding a long-neck bottle of Bud Light, approached him near the register.

"What in hell happened to you back there?" he asked T.J.

"I played hard."

"I guess. Streets is going to have to go home and reload his psyche."

"What about Tyron?" T.J. asked him.

"We'll see," Lindsey replied. "He played well, so we'll see. I'm still interested in what *you* did, though. I hope you're proud of yourself."

"I did what I had to do," T.J. answered immediately. He couldn't find significant pride in it, though. At least not yet. He looked directly into Lindsey's eyes before he said, "Isn't that what Full Court camp is for, Coach? Improvement?"

"I guess it is," said the coach, with a laugh.

Then T.J. had a question for Lindsey. "What was the commotion up there by the footbridge?"

"You mean the cop cars and the ambulance."

"Yeah. What was that about?"

"I'm not sure." Lindsey jerked his head in the direction of other coaches who were still at the far end of the bar. "Somebody said someone got killed over at that Bible camp."

"Who got killed?"

"I don't know. It could be just a rumor."

"What's the rest of the rumor?"

"The rumor is, some girl committed suicide."

T.J. found the rumor too disturbing. He paid for the gas but was distracted to the point he nearly forgot to get Tyron's snacks.

When he started the engine again, Tyron asked him, "Was Coach Lindsey in there?"

"You saw his car, Tyron; you know he was."

"What did Coach Lindsey say?"

T.J. lit a cigarette before he answered. "He said you played well."

"What about the scholarship, though?"

"He said we'll see."

"You mean he's going to call you?"

"No, Tyron. I mean he's going to call you."

NINE

AS soon as he got home, T.J. took all his dirty laundry and dumped it in a pile next to the washing machine. He was so tired he thought briefly about asking his mother to do the laundry for him, but even quicker did he realize what her answer would likely be: *Why would I do that? Is your arm broken?*

Upstairs, it was hot. He opened the windows in his room and lay in front of the twenty-inch fan, which he turned up to high. The air-conditioned dorm at Full Court had spoiled him. Nevertheless, his exhaustion was complete; he fell into a deep sleep that lasted most of the afternoon.

He watched the evening news while eating two bowls of Cocoa Krispies. Using the remote like a joystick, he surfed fretfully from one Peoria channel to another. They all reported the same event in essentially the same terms: a teenage girl from the Peoria area had fallen to her death at the Camp Shaddai Bible camp sometime just before dawn. Shelbyville County sheriff's deputies were joined in the investigation by state police. Foul play was not suspected, but circumstances of the death were unclear. The young woman's name was being withheld by authorities until such time as all family members had been notified. Film crews filed footage of the footbridge and the concrete steps approaching it while police personnel milled around, some of them in conversation while others walked around with their heads down as if searching for clues.

The beads of sweat that formed on T.J.'s forehead and upper lip were not merely from the heat. His stomach churned noisily. He was in the act of lighting up when his mother returned home from work. "You can't smoke in the house," was the first thing she said to him. "You should know that by now. Take it outside."

T.J. took it out on the porch. He finished the cigarette while the words of the anchorman replayed across his brain dramatically like one of those electronic message boards: *The young woman's name is being withheld until such time . . . the young woman's name is being withheld until such time . . .*

So distracted was he that when his mother joined him on the porch, it took a few moments before he realized he had company. She asked him how the basketball camp went. She had to ask a second time: "How did the camp go?"

"Oh, it was okay."

"That's all?"

T.J. was leaning against one post, his mother against the other. Their feet shared the same wooden step. "If you want the truth, it was a trip," he told her. "A real trip."

"I know it was a trip, but what was it like?"

"Not like that. I wouldn't know how to explain it."

"I hope you took care of Tyron."

"What's that supposed to mean?"

"He was a long way from home."

"So was I. So was everybody."

"You know what I mean. Some people are ready to take care of themselves and some people need someone watching over them."

"Tell me about it. Don't worry, I took care of him."

His mother sighed. She was rubbing lotion into her rough, red hands. Her veins were prominent. She was 110 pounds if she was lucky, T.J. thought to himself. *The young woman's name is being withheld until such time . . .*

"I'm still a little worried about how we're going to pay for it."

"I told you not to worry. We're not going to have to pay for it."

"I heard you before," she replied, "but I still look for the bill to show up in the mail. There's nothing free that I know of, so why should basketball camps be any different?"

"There won't be any bill in the mail," T.J. answered quickly. "It ain't gonna happen."

"Then who's paying your way? Who *paid* your way?"

"Coach took care of it. I'm not exactly sure how, but I don't think I want to know." If he told his mother that the money was probably routed through Coach DeFreese by way of Coach Lindsey's office at North State, it would only prolong a conversation he didn't want to pursue in the first place.

"I don't mean to hurt your feelings or anything, T.J., but the times I went to your games you didn't seem to be one of the main players. You were on the bench more than you were in the game."

"You're not hurting my feelings, Ma; don't worry about it." He really wanted to change the subject, but his mother beat him to it. She said, "I have to tell you that one of the houses on your route didn't get their paper this week."

"What house?"

"That adobe one over on Bradley Street. That huge dog was always in the front yard; I didn't want to get too close."

The huge dog she was talking about was a black Great Dane. He was ferocious in appearance, but not in fact. "They always keep him tied to a stake. He couldn't hurt you."

"And how was I supposed to know that? All I could see was this huge beast on his feet and moving toward me. How do you deliver the paper there?"

"I just throw it over the yard and onto the stoop."

"I'm not a thrower, T.J. Anyway, the people who live there are probably good and pissed. I wouldn't be surprised if they've been calling the newspaper office."

In his mind's eye, T.J. tried to picture his mother lobbing a folded-up newspaper thirty or forty feet over Mr. Levin's front yard, clear to the stoop. The thought made him giggle. He said, "I'll take care of it tomorrow, Ma. It won't be a problem."

"As long as you're taking care of things," she went on quickly, "you can also help me understand the last lesson they gave us on Quicken."

"What did they give you?"

"It was a lesson in shortcuts," she told him. "I get confused because they teach you a system using all the signs and words in the dialogue box, then they want you to ignore it all and use shortcuts."

"You'll get it okay; it's just a matter of practice."

"That's easy for you to say—you're young."

"You're young too," he reminded his mother.

"I'm old enough to be out of touch when it comes to computers, you can take my word."

"You're only thirty-five. You're young enough. Why not show me the lesson tomorrow? Maybe I can give you some help on it."

"I was hoping you'd say that," admitted his mother.

T.J. was staring up at the sky, which was turning dark, at the earliest stars making their appearance. The locusts were buzzing away loudly in their mindless mating chorus. It was different here at home than it was in the timber, yet it was the same. It might have been the same sky—*was* the same sky, in fact—and the same stars he'd pondered from the footbridge in the forest. He was relieved to be home, but not at peace. *The young woman's name is being withheld until such time . . .*

His mother stood up slowly and began brushing the seat of her blue jeans. She was going inside. Before she entered the house, T.J.

said to her, "I'm really exhausted, Ma. How'd you like to do my laundry for me?"

"Why would I do that? D'you have a broken arm or something?"

It wasn't until the following morning that T.J. was able to confirm what he'd feared, that the dead girl was indeed LuAnn. He read the story twice over on his knees while hunkered over the bundle of sixty-eight plastic-wrapped newspapers dropped for him on the corner. It was a prominent story on page three, a boxed article with a large headline. It was only five in the morning, so the light was pale, but there was enough to read by if he squinted.

The story said LuAnn Flessner fell to her death from the footbridge. Had there been more water in the gorge, suggested the sheriff's office, the fall most likely would not have been fatal. Preliminary reports fixed the time of LuAnn's death between two and four A.M. on the previous day. Investigators would try to discover the circumstances of the fall. Was it an accident? Was it suicide? Was she pushed?

An autopsy would be performed and a

coroner's jury would be convened to conduct an inquest. There wasn't much more information. T.J. knew, without thinking, that there would be subsequent articles and more thorough ones in other papers, the *Peoria Journal-Star* for instance.

He read the article one last time before loading the papers into his canvas shoulder bag and numbly folding the two or three nearest the top. He walked and folded by rote, nearly sleepwalking his way en route the long-familiar pattern of sidewalks and front porches and stoops and hallways. Full Court and Camp Shaddai and LuAnn Flessner seemed so far away and so long ago. And wasn't there even a sleazy guy, a street agent by the name of Bee Edwards? *Well, wasn't there?*

He tried not to, but he couldn't help but wonder if he had said any of the wrong things to LuAnn. Had he made too much fun of those religious beliefs that he found so naive? If she committed suicide, was his sarcasm something that added to her problems? He tried to replay in detail the conversations he'd had with her in his memory. Should he feel any guilt? Was there something wrong with him if he didn't?

The sun was up and there was early morning heat by the time he reached Levin's house. He was watering his front lawn. Hose in one hand and the leashed Great Dane in the other.

When T.J. approached to hand him the folded newspaper, the man said, "I didn't get my newspaper last week." He didn't say so in strident tones; he was very matter-of-fact about it.

"I know. My mother told me."

"I tried calling the office, but they weren't any help. It was five days I didn't get my paper at all. What's the story?"

"I was out of town. My mother took the route for me. She was afraid of your dog."

"The dog is always tied up. You know that."

"I know it, but my mother didn't," T.J. replied.

"Then you should have told her. That's what you have to do if you have someone substitute for you." Levin's dog was lying on his stomach and chewing aggressively on a huge rubber bone. Levin, himself, a wiry, hairy guy, was wearing shorts and a sleeveless Key Largo shirt. T.J. had conversed with him before a time or two, in this same flat monotone.

"Did you hear what I said?" Levin asked him.

"I heard you." Under other circumstances, T.J. might have found the man's displeasure a source of concern. But now he could only think of LuAnn and her long, swift free fall to the bottom of the gorge. The terror of the fatal impact and the instants before. He felt like telling Levin his missing newspapers weren't important. Instead, he said, "What would you like me to do about it now? Do you want me to get you the back issues, the ones you missed?"

"Why would I want to read old news?"

"I don't know. I'm askin' what you want me to do."

"You should get me a refund on my bill. That's what you should do."

"Okay, then," T.J. replied in a flat voice to match that of his dissatisfied customer, "I'll get you a refund." Then, without another word, he walked on. He needed to finish the route.

TEN

T.J. took a part-time job at Hardee's, working from three to seven, Sundays through
Thursdays. He was a lobby person. He washed
tables, took out trash, mopped floors, and
cleaned bathrooms. He didn't like the job, but
he wanted the cash, and it was a no-brainer;
after two or three days, the job itself was as
rote as his paper route.

Having the job meant spending less time
with Tyron, which was another benefit, as far
as he was concerned. There would be more
than enough time with the big guy once school
started.

Although his mother couldn't know it, he
planned to use some of the extra money to rent
computer time for her at Kinko's. One evening

when he returned home from work, she asked him how long he expected to keep the job.

"I don't know," T.J. replied.

"Are you going to work there after school starts?"

"Probably. I'll have to start later, though; school doesn't get out until 3:30."

"You have to have enough time for homework, T.J. You've got college in your future."

"I know, Ma."

"With your brains, you have to go to college. You can't ever forget that."

"I'm not forgetting."

"And what about basketball? What will you do when basketball practice starts?"

"I may keep the job, anyway," T.J. informed her. "I haven't made up my mind yet."

"You mean you might not go out for the team?"

"I haven't made up my mind yet," he repeated. "There won't be any practice till November, so I don't have to decide now."

By the middle of August, T.J. had a different mission for his diary. Instead of using it to record Bumpy's activities and inclinations where college recruiters might be concerned, he employed it now as a resting place for his own reflections and self-examination. At the top of one page in particular were the words *the unexamined life is not worth living*. He wasn't sure where he had heard this declaration—it probably came from Shakespeare or something—but he was convinced of its appropriateness.

He stapled together those pages that formed the first part, the section he had kept for the benefit of Coach Lindsey. They were sealed off then, but he decided against tearing them out and throwing them away. Someday, they might serve as a reminder of a lesson too important to forget.

Using the back cover of the diary because it was rigid, he paper clipped his saved newspaper articles dealing with LuAnn's death and the subsequent investigations into it. T.J. had not attended her funeral because it was a private one for family only. One of the articles was a profile of Brother Jackson, which characterized him as a "charismatic will-o-the-wisp evangelist." It revealed he was conducting revival meetings in Oklahoma at the time of her death.

The autopsy report revealed that LuAnn was pregnant, but there was no evidence of drugs in her system. The coroner's jury, which took three weeks to render a finding, determined that her death was a "simple suicide." No foul play was suspected.

Two other articles were interviews, one that quoted her family and schoolmates, and another that revealed the sorrow of her camp chums and counselor, Sister Simone, at Camp Shaddai. Sister Simone was quoted as saying. "Ruth Ann was a troubled but Spirit-led girl whose faith in the Lord was unconditional."

T.J. bought a Bible at a used-book store. He couldn't forget that last night in the wilderness when he'd had that final conversation with her, the one in which she disclosed to him her dream about the horse on the footbridge. He used a fresh page of the diary to write down some scripture: *When he opened the fourth seal, I heard the voice of the fourth living creature say, "Come!" And I saw, and behold, a pale horse, and its rider's name was Death, and Hades followed after him; and they were given power over a fourth of the earth, to kill with sword and with famine and with pestilence and by wild beasts of the earth.* T.J. wrote down Revelation, chapter and verse, but he had no idea what use, if any, he could ever make of this passage.

The 700 Club was on. From the corner of his eye he watched it on the small black-and-white TV located on an empty bookshelf. Sometimes he watched this program in the evenings, in spite of himself. There was something to learn, something perched only on the apron of his consciousness, but he felt it had something to do with the Rapture.

Once, while watching the program, he heard the Reverend Jerry Falwell say in an interview, "I expect never to die. His second coming is so imminent, I expect to join the Lord in the air. If you ever read an obituary of Jerry Falwell, rest assured that your surprise will be no greater than mine."

When he heard that declaration, T.J. couldn't help but think of the sermon he'd heard Sister Simone preaching that night in LuAnn's tabernacle. The language was so similar to these words out of the mouth of Jerry Falwell.

* * *

One day near the end of August, T.J. wrote in his diary that he was tired of manipulating. He didn't need to do that anymore. It wasn't necessary to spend your whole life guarded and wary and searching for methods of control. *A person can change*, he wrote in bold letters.

But he also wondered, change to what? A basketball star? Just because of that one shining moment at Full Court camp when he shut down Ronnie Streets? That was a moment driven more by guilty desperation than by any actual goal. In and of itself, how could it be the basis for any meaningful change?

He wrote in the center of a page, *I am a person in transition*. He might have written more, to attempt a framework for this change of life, but the phone rang. He had to go downstairs to the kitchen to answer it.

It was Gaines, the sportswriter. "You never called me about Full Court," he said.

"I never promised you I would."

"So how'd it go? Anything to report?"

"It would be old news now, wouldn't it?" said T.J. In his mind's eye he saw LuAnn and the footbridge, but he knew it wasn't the kind of material that the sportswriter sought. "Ishmael Greene is going to Notre Dame," he said.

"Everybody knows that," Gaines pointed out.

"Like I said, nothing to report."

As soon as he hung up, he saw the papers on the table, which were forms for school registration. There was also a note from his mother that said, *I signed these forms but I don't have time to fill them out. That's your job. Your work shirt is pressed in the second drawer. There's leftover casserole in the oven you can warm up.*

T.J. turned on the small TV that sat on the counter next to the stove. The news at noon from Channel 25 in Peoria was coming on as he fixed himself a grilled cheese sandwich. He looked at the registration forms briefly, but then Tyron was at the door. He joined T.J. at the kitchen table. He wanted to know if Coach Lindsey had called.

"If he calls," said T.J., "He'll be calling *you.*"

"Hows come?"

"Because I wrote him a note. I told him to take everything straight to you. Either you or Coach DeFreese."

"Hows come?"

"Because it's the right way. None of this shit needs to go through me anymore."

There was a large economy-size box of Famous Amos Oatmeal Cremes perched next to the newspaper. Tyron reached in to pull out five or six of the cookies. "But I want you to help me," he said.

"I didn't say I won't help you. If you want my advice, I'll give you advice. But nothing goes through me anymore, okay?"

"Jesus," muttered Tyron. His mouth was full. He was working his pick to fluff his 'fro, but it was with a searching look on his face, as if a thoughtful coiffing might help him absorb this change in strategy. Then he said, "You want to go to the arcade?"

"Not today. I have to work."

"I wish you didn't take that job, T.J. After work you wanta shoot?"

"Can we get in the gym?"

"We can get in. It's open gym tonight." Tyron

spoke with his mouth full; he was working on his second handful of the oatmeal cremes.

"You know, Tyron, if you get in a college program they're gonna want you in shape."

"I know. Lotsa time in the weight room. Lotsa lifting. I can handle that."

"Can you handle lots of lettuce and vegetables and fruit salad?"

"What d'you mean?"

"I mean coaches aren't going to want you eating cookies and Moon Pies and Whoppers with fries. They're going to want you in shape, maybe twenty pounds lighter."

"For real?"

"For real."

"That really sucks, T.J. In fact, that's double-suck."

"Maybe, but you need to know what you're gettin' yourself into."

Their conversation was interrupted when the sports came on. The lead story was Ishmael Greene's announcement that he would attend Notre Dame after graduation. On the screen were Ishmael, his parents, and his high school coach at a press conference. For style points,

Ishmael was wearing a Notre Dame hat.

When the reporter switched to the list of baseball scores, Tyron said, "Jesus, T.J. I can't believe he did it right in front of TV and everything."

"That would be Ishmael."

"I want to do that. Can I do that?"

"Do what? You're not thinkin' about Notre Dame again?"

"No, I wanna go on TV like that. I wanna go on TV and announce for North State."

"You can't do that now."

"Why?"

"Because they haven't even offered you a scholarship yet. A person can't announce where they're going until they get a scholarship offer."

"Maybe when I get the scholarship offer, then I can."

T.J. shrugged, then rubbed his eyes. *This has to be karma*, he couldn't help thinking. "Look, Tyron. Goin' on TV like Ishmael's doin' is just for show, you know what I mean?"

"No." As if for spite, he shoved two more cookies into his mouth.

"Ishmael's a *Parade* all-American. He's even a *USA Today* all-American. He loves the spotlight. But comin' on TV and sayin' that he's going to Notre Dame doesn't mean anything. Nothing's official until you sign your letter of intent, and you're not allowed to do that until November. You see what I mean? It's all for show."

"Then why's he doin' it if it doesn't mean nothin'?"

"Like I told you, because he loves the spotlight. That, and the fact that other recruiters will probably leave him alone now."

"I like it when recruiters call."

"I know you do."

The fatigue generated by this conversation was evident in Tyron's slumping body language. He said, "Okay, so what about the open gym? You wanta shoot?"

"What time is it open?" T.J. asked him.

"Six to ten."

"I don't get off till seven. I'll be there at seven-thirty."

"I wish you didn't take that job at Hardee's, T.J."

ELEVEN

THE first full day of school was on a Friday. To get through senior English with Mrs. Rubin, you had to start with *Hamlet*. Mrs. Rubin was a no-nonsense, old-line teacher without a surplus of patience.

To get to the back issues of area newspapers, which T.J. sought to do after school, you had to go through Rita Esposito, who was much younger than Mrs. Rubin in years, but not in behavior. Rita was the editor of the school newspaper, the *Herald*, as well as senior library aide for Mr. Hunter, the school librarian.

T.J. started by telling Rita he needed to search through some back issues of newspapers. "I'll be real careful not to mess them up," he promised.

"No can do, T.J. You have to write down the issues you want to see, and if we have them we'll bring them out to you."

"Come on, Rita; this is me, okay? I told you I'll keep them in order. Don't you trust me?"

"It's not a matter of trust," she said tersely. "It's a matter of procedures. Even if I wanted to let you back there, Mr. Hunter doesn't allow it."

They were standing at the reference desk, which formed a long U, at least fifty feet in its perimeter. T.J. could look from here through the windows, which formed part of the wall of the back issue room, where the newspapers were stacked on floor-to-ceiling bookcases. Rita's black hair was tied back severely into a tight ponytail. She wore little, if any, makeup and her horn-rimmed glasses were bent slightly askew. *Her officious behavior wouldn't go down any easier if she were a babe,* T.J. thought to himself. In fact, her colorless face and form fit the role she played perfectly.

"It's just that I'm not exactly sure what dates I need," he admitted. "If I could kind of sort through some of the back papers, I might be able to figure it out."

"Mr. Hunter used to let people *sort through* all the time," replied Rita quickly. "That's why the papers were always out of sequence or had parts missing. There's no point arguing this, because I don't make the rules. Here's a search form, if you want to fill it out." She pushed him a small white card that was clearly a refugee from the old card catalog.

T.J. took the card while he exhaled large in frustration. *There was no use arguing with the bitch, that was for sure. You give someone a little power, and then look what happens.* He went to the nearest table so he could sit down and rack his brain. The problem was, it had been more than a month since LuAnn's death. He could identify the exact day when the suicide occurred, but the follow-up and/or investigative articles he wanted to see could have been printed within days of her death or many days later. If it wasn't exactly that the trail was cold, by now it would surely be branched off in many directions.

There might be several newspapers in the mix. Articles could have been run in the Peoria paper, the Springfield paper, or even the

Chicago Tribune or *Sun-Times*. While T.J. was considering these possibilities, Rita came to take the seat beside him. "Get me the *Tribune* for the first week of August," he told her.

"You have to write it down," she replied. "Name of the paper and the dates you want. And no more than three issues at a time."

She is Mrs. Rubin in training, he thought. *She will probably skip her twenties and thirties and go straight into her forties.* He thought these thoughts, but wrote "*Chicago Tribune*, August 1, 2, and 3" on the card.

While Rita was locating the newspapers in the room with the windows, T.J. opened his copy of *Hamlet* and began leafing through the pages aimlessly. *To be or not to be . . .* He closed the cover just as quickly as he'd opened it. That had been the question for LuAnn, but she had chosen the wrong answer. Why, though? Why did she do that?

Rita brought him the three issues of the *Trib*, but it was no go. It didn't take long to review each newspaper because he could eliminate the sports and the business sections immediately. Then, it was just a quick flip through the front and the Tempo sections. He sent Rita back for August 4, 5, and 6.

But it was the same result: He came up empty. When he sent her back for the next three subsequent dates, she asked him, "How long does this go on?"

"I don't know. I can't say exactly what it is I'm looking for."

"No. Really?"

"Yeah, well, I guess that's what rules and regulations do for us. I told you I could save you a lot of work if you'd just let me look through on my own."

"Very funny." When she returned, she brought him a whole week's worth of *Tribunes*. "I'll never tell," T.J. promised.

"You better not." Rita returned to her computer behind the reference desk. T.J. didn't know her well, but well enough to know that she had very little life other than academics and the school paper. She was a loner and just nerdy enough to be picked on. Since it was Friday afternoon, the library was nearly empty; two students were working on computers located near the magazines, searching the Internet.

It took some time, but then he found an article that was right on target. More or less. It was a feature on religious cults, in the Tempo section, dated August 14. It was a long and thorough piece dealing with cults from various locations, but there were several references to LuAnn and Camp Shaddai along the way.

The writer pointed out how volatile the mix could be when there were unstable young people caught in the galvanizing group mentality of religious cults. One passage in particular that caught T.J.'s eye was a reference to LuAnn and depression. According to the writer, LuAnn was not only pregnant when she joined the troops at Camp Shaddai, she was under treatment for depression as well. But there were no specific details about the depression itself or what this *treatment* consisted of.

Perplexed, T.J. reread this passage a time or two before he continued to the end of the feature. The story quoted LuAnn's parents, in a later paragraph, as saying that membership in a religious cult was the one thing LuAnn didn't need, in her condition.

The word *cult*, T.J. thought to himself,

wouldn't go down very well with LuAnn herself or Sister Simone or other Camp Shaddai participants. It was a word that signified brainwashing or thought control, and they would all say that was nonsense, all they were doing was serving the Lord. But *depression*? How could she have been depressed? LuAnn was all smiles and serenity in her service to the Lord, wasn't she?

Rita was back at his table again. She had her elbows on the table and her chin cradled in her hands. She was staring at him. "It looks like you found what you wanted," she observed.

"I found something," he admitted. "I'm not sure if it's what I want."

"Have you ever thought about writing for the school paper?" she asked him.

"Why would I do that?"

"Oh, I don't know. You seem interested in newspapers, and you do have brains, T.J."

"Now you sound like my mother."

"I sound like everybody's mother," Rita responded.

T.J. wondered if that was why Rita was

staring at him, because she was hoping she might recruit him for the school newspaper staff. He tried to ignore her long enough to redirect his thoughts back to the Tempo feature. It still perplexed him, though; he decided he didn't know enough about depression.

"Do you know anything about depression?" he asked Rita.

"What are you asking me?" Her body language changed abruptly. She sat back in her chair and folded her hands in her lap.

"I said, do you know anything about depression?"

"Why would you ask me that? Why would you ask me that question?"

Rita's sudden change in behavior was startling to him. "Because I'm trying to figure something out in this article."

"But just right out of the blue, right out of nowhere, you ask me if I know about depression. Does that seem likely?" Rita's eyes were suddenly moist, as if she might be on the verge of tears.

"Jesus Christ, Rita, what's your agenda here? They're talking about depression in this article, and I'm asking you if you know any-thing about it. If you can't be cool with that, okay, but you can't be on my case about it."

"Does it seem like I'm on your case?" She stood up quickly and turned to leave. Before she headed in the direction of the reference desk, she added, "Just leave the papers where they are. I'll put them away later."

"Fuck your papers," said T.J. angrily, while turning away from her. He didn't get any of this. What did depression have to do with LuAnn Flessner and why was Rita Esposito pissed at him? Somewhere, somehow, there had to be something easy. He thought about the gym, where guys would be shooting by now. He decided to go and join them.

It wasn't until two weeks later that T.J found the time to return to the back issues of the newspaper in the school library. This time it was during his study hall, and Rita Esposito was nowhere in sight. He requested the same feature on cults he'd read before, and another library aide fetched it for him.

This time, before he read any further than

the headline, he made two copies on the Xerox machine, the second one darker and clearer than the first. It was at the table he was sharing with Tyron where he attempted to reread the feature from start to finish. But the big guy was keen on sharing something with him.

"How'm I gonna pass the ACT?" Tyron asked him.

It was a good question, T.J. thought, *as good as it always had been.* "You know I'm workin' on it, right? That's where we hope Mrs. Osby will help. That's what counselors are for." Having said this, and hoping it would close the discussion, T.J. returned to the photocopy of the news feature. There was a paragraph near the upper right corner that was too faint to read.

Tyron was squirming in his chair. He interrupted again with an announcement: "Anyway, I know what I'm gonna use for my term paper." He made this proclamation with a certain tone of defiance. "Look at this."

T.J. looked at the open book, a huge hardcover nearly the size of a road atlas, with page after page of color comic illustrations. "Okay,

I'm lookin', but keep your voice down, okay?"

"But look at this! You know what this is?"

By turning the cover, T.J. could read the title. *Encyclopedia of Super Heroes.* "You can't check this out, it's a reference book."

"I don't want to check it out, I'm gonna use it!"

"Use it for what?"

"For my report! For my term paper! Don't you get it?"

"Didn't I tell you to keep your voice down?" T.J. interrupted his thoughts long enough to rub his eyes. "Bumpy, this is a book about comic book heroes. This doesn't work for a history term paper. Mrs. Kemp won't okay it."

"That's what you think."

"That's what I know."

"You called me Bumpy."

"I'm sorry. I promised no more Bumpy. I don't want you to get your hopes up with a book about comic book figures."

Tyron adjusted his pick so that it extended from his afro at a more acute angle. He stood his ground uncharacteristically when he said,

"You think you know everything, but maybe you don't. Guess where I found this book."

T.J. glanced in the direction of the far end of the library, where the 600 stacks formed a T by joining with a lower counter. "Let me guess. The reference section?"

The big guy's flicker of disappointment was apparent, but short-lived. "Yeah, but you don't get it. That means nonfiction. I got this book in *nonfiction!*"

"SHHHHHHHHH! SHHHHH!"

T.J. looked both ways self-consciously, but he couldn't tell whether this shushing came from Mrs. Kemp or one of the librarians at the reference desk. He moved his face closer to Tyron's before he said, "Didn't I keep telling you to hold it down?"

"Okay, okay, but I found this book in nonfiction, which means it's real."

"What does that mean, *real*?"

"It means superheroes are real! People think they're just pretend, but they're not. They're real because they're in nonfiction!"

T.J. watched the eagerness spread across Tyron's face. Could Neal Armstrong's face have registered any more elation when he took his first step on the surface of the moon? *I got myself into this,* he reminded himself, *there's no one else to blame. He has to be encouraged, but there has to be some contact with reality.* Before he spoke, he let out a deep breath. "Tyron. Listen."

"I'm listenin'."

"There's reference books about everything. Gods, goddesses, evil spirits, nursery rhymes, leprechauns, et cetera et cetera. That doesn't make them real, just because they're in print."

"Miss Eades said fiction is false and nonfiction is true."

"Well, sort of, maybe. But not exactly."

"That's what she said."

"It's more like this: fiction stories are invented. They're made up. Reference books are books of information. You see the difference?"

What Tyron saw was the rising tide of disappointment. "Maybe I was the one listenin' to Miss Eades and not you."

T.J. couldn't argue with him, since he'd never had Miss Eades for English. "Maybe so, but I don't think you got the words quite right.

It's not the difference between true and false, it's the difference between information and made-up stories."

Even though Tyron had to know how reliable T.J.'s understanding of these matters usually was, he was reluctant to let this one go. "I don't have to take your word for it," he said.

"That's true."

"I don't have to take your word for it." Tyron repeated the words, but his quieter voice betrayed his sense of resignation. "I can still ask Mrs. Kemp about it."

"Yeah, you can do that," said T.J.

"That's probably what I'll do."

"Do me a favor, Tyron. Take the pick out of your hair, okay?"

"No." Tyron rested his head on his arms. He was so huge that in this position he covered most of the table. "We're gonna shoot tonight, remember?" he asked. His voice was muffled by the crook of his left elbow.

"Not until after seven-thirty, though. Remember?"

"Yeah, I remember. I wish you never took that job at Hardee's, T.J."

"Most of the time, so do I. I guess we both wish it."

By the time T.J. got to the gym after work, it was crowded. In addition to little kids who were playing on the decks, the main gym was peopled by players from the other high schools in town, as well as his own. He got into a pickup game with Tyron on his team, as well as two guys from West High. He couldn't help thinking, for the umpteenth time, how odd it was to be friends with players most of the year, and then turn them into enemies as soon as the season started. It wasn't natural.

T.J. didn't think about it for long. He made six jump shots in a row, pure, with elevation he didn't normally have and high extension with his arms. The ball rolled from his fingertips with proper rotation. His swishing shots hardly touched the rim.

Before long he was whipped, though. He sat on the first row of bleachers, gasping for breath, when Coach DeFreese took the seat next to him. It wasn't legal for the coach to actually instruct the players, in any organized context, before November first. But it wasn't against the rules to watch and give tips or advice to individuals.

"Why are you so bushed?" he wanted to know.

"I'm not that tired," T.J. lied. "I just want to give other guys a chance to play."

"You're not still smokin' those Marlboros, are you?"

"Who, me, Coach? Never."

"Good-lookin' jump shot tonight. Did they work you on that at Full Court?"

"No, Coach," T.J. replied haltingly though his gasps for breath. "They taught me other things."

"Good," said the coach. "Anything you learn will help."

It would be a waste of breath to try to explain to the coach what he meant. And he didn't have any breath to spare, at this point in time. "God, Coach, I *love* this game," said T.J., speaking like a parrot echoing the slogan of the NBA promotional television spots.

"Are you coming out for the team, then?"

"Don't know yet; haven't made up my mind."

"Why not? I thought you said you loved this game."

"I do. This game tonight, right here and right now. I love it. As for the team, I need to think about it. I'd have to quit my job."

"You know, Nucci, you're a spook sometimes. You know that?"

The coach left after delivering this observation. T.J. could ignore him with no difficulty. He was watching Tyron slam home a rebound and punch his fist in the air triumphantly. *Superman is real,* thought T.J. *People think superheroes are pretend, but they're really not.*

With his breathing restored, T.J. seemed to recover most of his brain. The thing with Tyron was more than he could process by himself. He needed advice. The only person he could think of whose input might be valuable was Mrs. Osby.

TWELVE

THE day Tyron showed him the letter from Coach Lindsey was the third day in a row T.J. had postponed talking to Mrs. Osby. The letter said:

> *Dear Tyron:*
> *Due to recent developments*
> *since the conclusion of Full Court*
> *camp, we find we will be unable*
> *to offer you a basketball scholar-*
> *ship this year at North State. We*
> *are sorry to have to tell you this,*
> *but we are confident you will find*
> *a situation at another school that*
> *will suit you better. Thank you for*
> *your interest in us. We wish you*
> *the best of luck.*

Coach Lindsey's signature was at the bottom.

Tyron was crestfallen. "Does this mean for sure I won't get a scholarship?"

T.J. read through the letter a second time before he answered. "Yeah, Tyron, that's what it means."

"But they promised."

"More or less they did, but not in writing."

"They promised if I passed the ACT I'd get the scholarship."

T.J. could have told Tyron he was surprised by this turn of events, but he'd be lying if he did. "They promised you, but not in writing. A scholarship offer isn't official till they give you a letter of intent to sign."

"So what does that mean?"

"It means they broke their word, but there's nothing to be done about it. They're within their rights."

"Shit," said Tyron. "What does this mean here, *recent developments over the summer?*"

"I can't say for sure. It probably means they found somebody else." *Somebody who doesn't represent so much work,* T.J. thought to himself, *somebody who isn't a* project.

"Jesus."

"I'm sure it happens all the time, Tyron, don't feel too bad. There's other colleges, there's even lots of junior colleges."

"Yeah, but I want to play for the Vultures." He slumped dejectedly against the post that supported him on T.J.'s front porch.

"I know, Big Guy. I'm sorry." And indeed he was. There wasn't time to indulge it now, however. "I have to go to work, Tyron. I'll see you later."

The next morning, T.J. sucked it up and went to see Mrs. Osby. He made an appointment during his study hall. He told her about the letter in which North State had withdrawn the scholarship offer to Tyron.

"That's too bad," said the counselor. "But isn't it true that he's had letters of interest from many other schools?"

"That's true, but lots of the time the letters are just letters. They get sent to hundreds of players on a mailing list. It doesn't prove that a college has any real interest. I've even gotten a few myself since Full Court camp."

"It still doesn't seem like a big problem, T.J." Mrs. Osby spoke firmly, but her tone of voice was reassuring. She sat up very straight and laced her fingers on her desk blotter. "Because of basketball, his opportunities after graduation will still exceed those of other students who might have similar academic limitations."

What she said was true, but it missed the point. Or points. "They did give their word, though."

"They promised him a scholarship?"

T.J. nodded. "It was only verbal, though; nothing in writing. And it was only if he qualified academically."

"If they broke their word, that's regrettable, but I would assume that in the world of big-time college athletics, there would be no shortage of broken promises. Would I be wrong?"

"No, you would be right." The next thing would be, how much could he share with her? She wasn't the kind of person you could enjoy, but her sincerity was something to respect. It wouldn't be hard to trust her, but getting in a comfort zone would be something else. He said, "Ever since I read the letter, I've wanted to get back at them. It's like I've wanted to find a strategy for revenge."

"Revenge? What would provoke you to want revenge?"

T.J. took a deep sigh, but then he went ahead and told her the whole story. He summarized his meetings with Lindsey, the journal/diary he'd been keeping, the implied payoff he might receive for his record keeping, and the fact that he went to Full Court only to protect his interest in Tyron. When he was finished with the summary, he said, "Which brings me to the subject of the ACT."

"What about the ACT?" Mrs. Osby asked.

"I don't want you to read it to him," said T.J. bluntly.

"And why not?"

"Because the whole thing is phony. It's part of this whole stupid game. The idea came from Lindsey, not from me. It was part of the 504 strategy. See, it's like everything about this is strategy, not honesty."

Mrs. Osby straightened her posture even more erect before she answered. "Can't you see anything positive in all this, T.J.?"

"Positive? About what?"

"About yourself. Can you see any sense in which Tyron is better off because of your interest in him?"

"Not right now. Right now I can't."

"He's a better player because of you. He's a better student because of you. He has goals. He's less susceptible to gang or drug cultures because of you. Please tell me if I'm wrong."

It was a liberating feeling, something honest, something pure, to have a discussion like this one, with no cover-your-own-ass political motivation. T.J. wondered how it was Mrs. Osby could combine so much formality with trustworthiness. It crossed his mind that the other part of his dilemma, the LuAnn part, was a subject he could discuss with her. But that conversation, if it ever came, would have to wait till another day. T.J. said, "With all due respect, Mrs. Osby, you're sounding a little bit like those arguments the college coaches use."

"How's that, T.J.?"

"They say Tyron will be better off in college than out of it, even if he doesn't graduate. He spends four years playing basketball, which he loves, and the chance for an education is always there."

"What else do coaches say?"

"They say if he never graduates, and ends up at Burger King the rest of his life, it's still the same result, only at least he doesn't have to flip burgers straight out of high school. He gets the four years of glory and he's no worse off."

"Does any of that make sense to you?"

"In a way," T.J. had to admit, "but it seems pretty lame. It's like a cop-out. I should know. The bottom line is, my biggest reason for getting involved with Tyron and North State was for myself. I thought it would make me important. I thought I could have big-time power with college coaches. I've been using him. I hate to put it this way, but the fact is I turned myself into a street agent."

"I'm not sure what a street agent is, but I do know that none of us has pure motivations. We all do things for a mixture of reasons, especially those things we feel are important. I hope someday you'll understand that part of what motivates you is affection for Tyron, and a concern for his best interests."

"I can only appreciate that in my head, not where my feelings are concerned."

"Then maybe someday. Maybe a month from now, or two months from now."

"Maybe," T.J. mumbled without conviction.

Mrs. Osby took her glasses off. She began to clean them, using a bottle of Lenspure. When she finally spoke, she said, "If you think the ACT is part of the problem, I can tell you how to solve that."

"What should I do?" T.J. asked.

"Don't do anything," Mrs. Osby replied.

"Do nothing?"

"No. Let me decide. It may be that Tyron is a student with an undiagnosed disability who needs to have the test read to him, or it may not. Let me decide."

"I suppose so." He was surprised at the relief he felt, but it made perfect sense.

"That's what I get paid for. I have more background than you do, so let me decide. You wrote that coach and told him not to include you in the loop any more. I'm giving you permission to let this testing part of it go."

T.J. felt silly enough that he could only repeat himself. "I suppose so."

When he stood up to leave, T.J. shook her hand. "Are you a good player too, T.J.?" Mrs. Osby asked him.

"I was once," he replied.

"Do you mean you used to be?"

"No, I mean I was once."

The revenge factor didn't go away immediately. T.J. longed to get back at someone, somehow, even when he understood his anger was mostly directed at himself. As disturbed as Tyron might have been about the letter, T.J. was no less disturbed, if in a different way. The letter seemed to add defeat to treachery. While he tied off plastic bags of trash and wiped Formica tabletops in Hardee's lobby, his inner dialogue crafted a fantasy of revenge. He knew he had power he could use if he chose to:

This is the story that Gaines, the sportswriter, wants. If I showed him the diary, he would pay money for it. It would only be a question of how much. It would be a lot simpler, though, to just go to Lindsey and threaten to do it. Something

*like, if you pull Tyron's scholarship offer, I go to
Gaines with the diary, and he writes feature articles about it. It would be blackmail, but North
State would be between a rock and a hard place.
They wouldn't have a choice. They would end
up paying me the money and giving Tyron the
scholarship as well.*

As foolproof as it seemed, T.J. knew immediately how much it sucked. While he was
heaving full bags of trash into the stinking
Dumpster, he reminded himself, *And then
what? More political bullshit, more guilt. If
you found what looked like a window of
opportunity, it was really a trapdoor, so you
had to put all your energy into looking for the
next door and trying to find out what it would
take to open it. A vicious circle without an
end.* He shook his head.

When he went inside to wash up and change
out of his uniform shirt, he saw Rita Esposito.
She was sitting by herself in one of the corner
booths, the one farthest away from the counter.
It wasn't hard to pick her out because the crop of
customers was thin; by this time of the evening
most of the supper surge was on the wane.

T.J. hadn't seen her since that day in the library a few weeks earlier when she sort of spun out on him. There wasn't any reason to think that she was here to see him, although it was unusual for her to show up at Hardee's.

When he emerged from the bathroom, having washed up and changed into his Bulls jacket, Rita was looking at him. He approached her table. "Yo, Rita; what's up?"

"I thought maybe we could talk for a few minutes," she replied. Rita had a notebook with unruly pages sticking out and two college catalogs on the table in front of her, Northwestern and the University of Missouri.

"Why not? I was going to get some coffee before I leave. You want a cup?"

"You buying?"

"Let's say I am."

"Okay, I'll take one. One sugar, please, no cream."

When T.J. returned with the coffees, he asked Rita about the catalogs.

"I'm either going to Northwestern or Missouri," she told him. "It'll depend on the aid package I can get. They're both expensive, though. Missouri because it would be out-of-state tuition and Northwestern just because it's expensive."

"With your grades and résumé, you could probably get a scholarship to Yale if you wanted."

Rita took a sip of the coffee before she answered. Her glasses were slightly askew. She must have had corn for supper, because there was a small husk clinging to one of her front teeth. "I've checked into Yale," she said. "It's not good enough."

T.J. found this to be a choice remark. "Why isn't it good enough?"

"It isn't rated that high for journalism. I want the best journalism school I can find. The best one in the East would probably be Syracuse, but I have no desire to go there."

"It must be nice to have your future so figured out."

"When your present is unpleasant, you tend to concentrate on your future." She said this to him while staring directly into his eyes, over the rim of the steaming coffee cup.

T.J. thought he understood what she meant.

She was talented and brilliant, but she was also a nerd. Most people didn't like her; they made fun of her. She probably would be a lot better off in a college setting. But even though he thought he understood, he couldn't think of anything to say.

"What about you, T.J.?" Rita inquired. "What are your plans for college?"

"I don't have any yet. I might even go to junior college. I need to start thinkin' about it, though."

"Have you got your paper done for Mrs. Rubin yet?"

T.J. didn't answer right away. He wondered by this time why Rita wanted to talk to him, anyway; it couldn't be just to gab about colleges and papers for English class. Or could it? He even wondered how she knew where he worked and what time he got off. He finally said, "No."

"What are you writing it on?"

"I haven't started yet. When I do, I'm going to write about Hamlet."

"Is that supposed to be funny?"

"No. Why?"

"Because everybody has to write about

Hamlet; that's the play we're reading."

"I don't mean about the play," said T.J. "I'm just going to write about Hamlet himself, the main character. Just *him*, just the *guy*. I understand him all the way down."

"And why is that?" Rita took a cigarette from her purse and started to light it.

"You better not smoke that in here," he warned her, "I've had the manager on my case for smokin' even in the entryway."

She blew a smoke ring. "I'll take my chances."

"I'm warnin' you, though."

"I know. I heard the warning. I asked you why you think you understand Prince Hamlet so well."

"Because he's all fucked up inside and doesn't know what to do. He thinks this way, then he thinks that way. He thinks he's got something figured out but then it's like something puts him back to square one. He's in over his head and it makes him paralyzed."

"Wow," whispered Rita, clearly impressed. "Have you been there?"

"I've been there," T.J. replied quickly. But at this point he was running out of patience, besides which, her smoking made him nervous. Someone could come back here and kick them out. "Rita, why'd you want to talk to me, tell me that."

"Okay."

"I can't believe you want to tell me about college catalogs or find out what I'm writing for my English paper."

"Right. Okay. You asked me about depression, but I came unglued."

"Yeah, I remember."

"Well, I'm okay with it now. What did you want to know?"

This was a surprise; it took him a few moments to collect his thoughts before he explained, "I knew the girl who died at the Bible camp. The one who committed suicide. You know who I'm talkin' about?"

"A little bit. It was in all the papers. She was from Peoria."

"Yeah, okay. Her name was LuAnn. I was at basketball camp in the same complex. I talked to her a few times. It was just by accident that we met at all, but we talked about some personal stuff."

"You're sad that she died."

"Yeah, but what I was askin' you that day was about depression. An article I read in the *Trib* said she was being treated for depression before she went to the Bible camp. That really confused me."

"Why? If a girl commits suicide, why would it be a surprise to find out she was depressed?"

"Because she was all smiles and grins. She was all happy in the Lord, and joining the Lord in the air for the Rapture."

"You think she couldn't be depressed if she smiled all the time?"

"Well, yeah. It makes sense, doesn't it?" If his remark was naive, T.J. didn't know why.

Before she answered, Rita dropped her cigarette, which was half smoked, into the coffee cup, which was still half full of liquid. They both listened to the *sizzz*. "Let me tell you what I know. I spent six weeks this summer in County West. I assume you know what that is."

T.J. did know. County West was the psych unit. "I know what it is."

"While you were shooting baskets," she continued, "I was being probed and stuck and serving as a guinea pig for various medications."

"Rita, why are you telling me this?"

"Maybe I want us to be better friends, so I can talk you into writing for the paper." She was smiling, for the first time. The small corn husk was gone now, so maybe the coffee had rinsed it off.

"I didn't ask you about depression to pry into your personal life."

"I know you didn't. It's not a problem. I'm okay with this now. I've got the right medication, so I'm good. What I can tell you is this: I got to know a lot of people with acute depression. Some of them smiled a lot."

"They did?"

"Some of them did. There were others who were all melancholy and miserable, including me. But some people you'd never know, not by their appearance or their behavior."

"But why would that be?"

"I can't say for sure. Sometimes it seems like it's a mask, but other times it seems to be like a form of denial. Just make believe you're happy and sooner or later you'll have yourself convinced."

T.J. leaned back in his chair and stretched

his arms above his head. This was food for thought. Even with all the smiles and the rose-colored lenses, LuAnn might have been in depression, even the acute kind. Rita Esposito wasn't sweet or charming, but she was a person you could believe if she told you something.

Rita was putting on her coat. "I have to get going," she told T.J. "But before I do, there's one other thing I'm thinking of about your friend."

"Yeah, what's that?"

"Some of those wackos in a religious cult would probably tell her she didn't need to take medication. That's even if she *was* taking any, which I'm sure we don't know; but if she was, they might've told her that people who have to take medication for emotional problems are just proving they don't have enough faith in the Lord."

"You mean like there's no need to take medicine because the Lord will satisfy all your needs."

"That's what I'm saying. If that's what happened, then your friend could have been not only depressed, but off her medication. It's just a thought."

"And that could affect her behavior? If she quit taking her medication, I mean."

"Oh, no more than a diabetic who stops taking their insulin," was her sarcastic response.

"Why do you have to be such a smart-ass? I'm just asking you a question."

"Sorry. But, yes. Not only her behavior, but possibly her judgment and even her decisions. That's all I'm saying."

"And all I'm saying is, if you sanded off some of your rough edges, you might make a few more friends."

"That's a charming thought, but rough edges is who I am." It was Rita's last word on the subject, just before she headed out the door.

For a few moments, T.J. tried to absorb the information she'd given him. By hurrying after her, though, he caught up before she pulled her car out of the parking lot. "I was just thinkin', Rita. You really want me to write for the school paper?"

"Sure. Are you interested?"

"I'll think about it," he answered. "Not makin' any promises, but I'll think about it."

THIRTEEN

THIS time the road was beautiful. There was scarlet sumac in the ditch next to the shoulder, and the timber was transformed by an October palette of gold and orange maple leaves splashed against the brown oak. The visibility was better too. Enough leaves had fallen to provide open spaces for viewing clear to the shining reservoir.

T.J. drove slowly, relishing this same environment that had seemed such a forbidding wilderness the first time he'd traveled it. The road wasn't any wider or any straighter, but it felt opened up. A warm sun perched high in the sky of bluest blue and shimmered on the wet blacktop.

He parked on the other side of the complex

this time, in the lot near the administration building next to the section where LuAnn's camp had been housed. There were puddles in the gravel lot from last night's rain.

Sister Simone began the conversation by telling him she sold Mary Kay Cosmetics. "When I'm not involved with Camp Shaddai," she added.

T.J. could believe it. Her own makeup was expert. She was a beautiful woman for some-one in her thirties or maybe as old as forty. Even her body was primo; she had clear skin and a golden brown tan.

"You caught me just in time," she told him. "After October, we're in recess until the spring. By next week at this time, I'll be back in Chicago."

They were sitting in an open shelter, on a wooden bench with an uncomfortable back. It was probably a place where LuAnn had gloried in one of the many praise meetings. It wasn't too different, only a little smaller, from that other tabernacle place. The one he'd stumbled into in the dark back in July, when he'd observed Sister Simone preaching to the flock.

From this position, T.J. could see the large lake and spillway out to the west, through the silvering leaves of the cottonwoods. But he couldn't see the courts where they had had their games, or the footbridge. There was still too much foliage blocking the view. Maybe in December, he thought, you'd be able to see clear across, but who'd want to sit outdoors in the winter?

"Did you know Ruth Ann well?" Sister Simone asked him.

T.J. resisted the urge to substitute her real name. Maybe, considering all the different sides she had, and her troubled past, maybe it was Ruth Ann he had known after all. "Yes and no," he said.

"Yes and no?"

To clarify, T.J. summarized his week at Full Court and the meetings he'd had with LuAnn on the bridge. While he was doing so, it occurred to him that if that spillway overflowed, it would, in effect, have a flooding effect that would back water into the gorge. If so, jumping from the bridge might not kill you. And wasn't that an observation made by one of the sheriff's deputies in a newspaper article he'd read?

"You said LuAnn," Simone observed, with a smile.

"I did?"

"Yes." The counselor paused before she continued. "I feel we honor her better by calling her Ruth Ann, since it was the name she chose after she was baptized in the Spirit. It symbolized her surrender to the Lord."

"Whatever," said T.J. without enthusiasm. "I was just thinking that the only place I ever talked to her, the only place I even saw her, was on that footbridge."

"The Lord works in mysterious ways, His wonders to perform."

T.J. lit a cigarette, but Simone said, "I wish you wouldn't smoke that."

"Yeah, me too. But it's a free country, and we're outdoors."

When she spoke next, her tone of voice was terse: "Is there something I can do for you, C.J.?"

"It's not C.J., it's T.J." *Did this woman have a thing for changing people's names?*

"Very well, then, T.J. If there's something I

can do for you, please tell me what it is. I have another appointment later this afternoon and I'll need some time to get ready for it."

"Well, it might be that I came here to confess."

"Confess?"

"Yeah, maybe so. You're a counselor, right? Maybe the first thing is, I came so I could confess how I used Bumpy at basketball camp."

"I would have no idea what you're talking about," said Sister Simone. Her facial expression was benign, but her eyes were impatient.

"Yeah, well, I used him. Just trust me on it. I pretended like I was helping him, but I was really trying to goose up my own status."

"Whatever this means, it's apparently something you've reconciled in your own heart. I'm sure the Lord will bless you for it."

"Please don't say that," T.J. objected.

"What would you like me to say," asked Sister Simone, "with so little information?" This was just a rhetorical question, obviously, because she moved quickly to the next one: "You said that was the first thing. Is there a second thing?"

"Yeah, there is." T.J. was surprised how he didn't feel nervous, even though he expected he would be. "I thought maybe you might like a chance to confess."

"What did you say?"

"Confessing is good for us, right? I thought maybe you might have something you'd like to 'fess up about LuAnn's suicide."

"This is astonishing. Who do you think you're speaking to?"

"There's a chance this is nutso," T.J. was willing to admit. He stepped on his cigarette to put it out.

"What on earth do you think you know about Ruth Ann's death?" the counselor demanded. "Or her life, for that matter?"

"I know it probably sounds weird, but the more I think about it, the more I *do* know. I know she was pregnant, and I know who Brother Jackson was. Is. It wouldn't surprise me if he was the father."

"Do you have any information to that effect?"

"No."

"I thought not. The other information you

mention was in the newspapers. Even a casual reader would know it."

"I did keep all the newspaper articles I could find, but I know a lot of other stuff too. I know about her dreams, especially the one about the pale horse running on the foot-bridge. I know the Bible passage it comes from. I even know she was going to ask you to interpret the dream."

"I thought you said you didn't know her very well." Sister Simone's discomfort wasn't revealed by her face, but for the first time she was engaging in some restless body language.

"Actually, I said yes and no, remember? Looking back, I'd say the two of us did a lot of communicating in a short time. She even told me a lot about you."

"You are the most astonishing person." She was picking at lint on her navy blue slacks. If there was any there, though, T.J. couldn't see it.

"I'm not usually this way, because I'm too careful," T.J. said. "But I think you could have prevented her death if you'd had the guts."

"What did you say to me?"

"I think when she came to you with the dream about the pale horse, you didn't have the guts to tell her to forget about it. You could have told her to kiss it off and go to sleep. Instead, she probably asked you something funky like wasn't the devil's child inside of her or something. So wasn't the dream of death a sign from God?"

"How dare you presume about the nature of our conversations?!"

"How do I, that's a good question. Anyway, you could have told her to go to bed, or go home and work things out with her parents, but what's the kick in that? It's like there wouldn't be any *Rapture*. I think you people play the God game, where the things people do have to fit in with your rules, or else they don't count."

Sister Simone was on her feet. "You are the most presumptuous, impertinent person. I can only think that for some reason the Lord must want you to say these things."

"All I know is, *I* want to say them. If I'm wrong, you can tell me, but I think she asked you if the dream was a sign of death that came from God. You probably didn't tell her yes or no. You probably gave her something real lame, like, 'Who can say, Ruth Ann? The Lord speaks to every one of us in a different way.'"

"I don't have to listen to this," declared Simone. It was evident she would have left immediately, but there were manila folders she had to stuff carefully into an overburdened shoulder bag. If she did it recklessly, the papers would fall out.

"Even if the Lord wants me to say it?" asked T.J. "I could be wrong, but I guess the Rapture kick was more important than LuAnn was. That's how you used her."

"If you haven't noticed, I'm not listening anymore. I have to go."

"That way you could do what you wanted for the purpose of the God game, but still pretend like LuAnn did everything on her own. You don't have to take responsibility, you're off the hook. If you think about it, it's a little bit like me and the basketball camp."

She was shouldering the bag. "If your impertinence wasn't bad enough, now you want to draw some parallel between some common basketball camp and service to the Lord God and His kingdom."

"Like I said, you can tell me if I'm wrong."

Her back was turned. "I don't intend to tell you anything," she announced. Then she left, without looking back.

T.J. watched Sister Simone for the length of time it took her to disappear. It was surprising how little emotion he felt in the aftermath of this encounter. He had brought her face-to-face with a serious charge, yet he felt almost none of the stress associated with a confrontation.

He knew he was right, that his reconstruction of the God game scenario featuring LuAnn and Sister Simone was accurate. There was no way of proving it, of course, but some things you just knew. So where, then, was the thrill of victory? What about the rush of vindication?

He walked slowly to the bridge, clear to the center, where he rested his forearms on the rough railing. It was a splinter that had brought them together in the first place. He was sorry he hadn't known LuAnn Flessner better, sorry she was dead, and sorry he hadn't been able to attend her private funeral.

For all the sorrow, though, the mystery was what she meant to him in fact, or he to her. He couldn't really say that he enjoyed her. The truth was, he probably would have *enjoyed* the "old" LuAnn more, the girl who hadn't been saved and sanctified.

T.J. looked down at the spot where she probably died, where the dry gorge reached its deepest point. All he could see were the rocks themselves, groups of sticks caught in the crevices between, and a few dirty, mangled soft drink cans. He hoped she died right away, without having to lie there suffering.

He thought he ought to be able to say what it was that linked their two lives however briefly. There had to be words for it. *Down was death, up was Heaven,* he thought to himself. *South was Shaddai, north was Full Court, east was the way back home, and west, if he stood here long enough, would be the setting sun.*

EPILOGUE

IT took him two hours to put on the new alternator, or about twice as long as it should have. The bolts were rusty and the new alternator, which wasn't new at all but a rebuilt one, had irregular brackets. Even so, he was finished before his mother got home from work.

She took off her coat, got seated at the kitchen table with the newspaper, and asked T.J. how he'd like some macaroni and cheese with cut-up hot dogs for supper.

"Don't get too comfortable," he told her. "I want to take you out to the mall for a little while."

"You must have the car running again."

"Yeah, it's fixed. All the skin that used to be

on my knuckles should grow back real soon."

"So why do you want to go to the mall? What's out there?"

T.J. was leaning against the kitchen sink, peeling a banana. "I'm going to buy you a computer," he said matter-of-factly.

His mother was in the process of hunting for the crossword. She looked up from her newspaper to say, "You're going to buy me a computer? What kind?"

"A Mac Performa, of course. A Power Mac. You do want to work on Quicken, don't you?"

"Did you win the lottery or something?"

He spoke as distinctly as he could with his mouth full. "Nope, no lottery. I want you to get your coat on."

"I just took it off. If they're paying you that much money at Hardee's, maybe I should go to work there."

"They aren't paying me anything at Hardee's. I quit."

"When did you quit?"

"Last week. Get your coat on."

"This really sounds crazy, T.J."

"Crazy as it oughta be, that's how I see it. Now put your coat on."

They drove east toward Veterans Parkway. His mother was trying to use the small mirror on the visor to apply some lipstick. It wasn't easy, because the ride was a rough one. "Why did you quit your job?" she asked him.

"So I can go out for basketball. Practice starts next week."

"I'm glad, T.J."

"I know you are. I guess I am too."

"I'm glad," she continued, "because you need more friends and more activities. It's good for you."

"That's not why I'm doin' it, though, Ma." It would probably please her just as much, or maybe more, to hear that he was going to start writing for the school newspaper.

"Why are you doing it, then?"

"Because I think I can be a good player. In fact, I think I *am* a good player."

"I guess you must be, or they wouldn't have wanted you in that big-shot summer basket-ball camp."

T.J. sighed before he answered. "We've been

all over that before; there's nothin' else to say about it." He was maneuvering into the exit lane that led to the mall parking lot. "I'll miss the money, though."

"You've still got the paper route. That should get you by."

"But the paper route only pays sixty dollars a week."

"I know how much it pays," she reminded him. "If you keep your needs simple, that's plenty of money."

"My needs are real simple," he declared. He found a parking spot close to JCPenney's and shut off the engine. "It's this car," he added, while slapping the steering wheel for emphasis, "that has expensive tastes."

Once in the mall, he took her to Kinko's. His mother admitted to him she didn't know Kinko's sold computers, to which he answered, "They sell computers by the hour, Ma. I'm going to buy you a Mac for an hour, or maybe even two, if you get into the flow."

She was nodding her head. "I get it now. We're going to rent the Mac."

"Buy, rent, whatever. Why don't we take the

one down there on the end, the Power PC in the 6100 series."

They booted up the Quicken program. She found her way into a standard payout chart, but when she wanted to move from field to field, she struggled clumsily with the mouse to set the cursor.

"You can move from field to field with the tab key," T.J. told her. "It's a lot easier than messin' around with the mouse. And it's faster too."

"That's what they were trying to teach us in class."

"Well, they were right. Just hit the tab key and it moves the cursor to the next field."

She did as he advised, but then complained. "Now it's in the debit column, which is what I don't want."

"Then tab it again." He watched her fingers working the keyboard. It wasn't the first time he'd noticed how long her fingers were, especially for such a small person. Her nails were uneven, but they were clean. When the cursor moved swiftly to the column she wanted, she leaned back in her chair and beamed, a wide smile spreading across her face like a child who gets an A on a spelling test.

"You could move to the fields down on the next level this way?"

"Exactly. It's that easy."

"You are a good boy, T.J.," she declared.

"Don't I know it, Ma. Ain't it the truth."

Exciting fiction from three-time Newbery Honor author
Gary Paulsen

Newbery Honor Book

TRACKER

Newbery Honor Book

DANCING CARL

SENTRIES

Simon & Schuster Children's Publishing Division
where imaginations meet
www.SimonSaysKids.com